VACATIONLAND

CHRISTOPHER CORBETT

VACATIONLAND

V I K I N G

VIKING
Viking Penguin Inc., 40 West 23rd Street,
New York, New York 10010, U.S.A.
Penguin Books Ltd, Harmondsworth,
Middlesex, England
Penguin Books Australia Ltd, Ringwood,
Victoria, Australia
Penguin Books Canada Limited, 2801 John Street,
Markham, Ontario, Canada L3R 1B4
Penguin Books (N.Z.) Ltd, 182–190 Wairau Road,
Auckland 10, New Zealand

First published in 1986 by Viking Penguin Inc.
Published simultaneously in Canada

LIBRARY OF CONGRESS CATALOGING IN PUBLICATION DATA
Corbett, Christopher.
Vacationland.
I. Title.
PS3553.06437V3   1986   813'.54   85-31470
ISBN 0-670-80322-7

Printed in the United States of America by
R. R. Donnelley & Sons Company, Harrisonburg, Virginia
Set in Goudy
Design by Jacqueline Schuman
Title typography by William Sloan

For Rebecca and my parents

Due to the unfortunate tendency among many authors to claim that their works are fiction when in fact they are based on actual events and real people, it should be noted here that the following account is in fact based entirely on actual events and real people.

All of the following things actually took place not very long ago as they are set down here, and all of the people, places and things herein exist. This is the whole truth and nothing but the truth.

If in consulting a map or atlas of Maine the reader is unable to find some of the places referred to herein, please understand that the author assumes no responsibility for faulty maps and atlases.

It should be noted that the most recent edition of the state highway map of Maine inadvertently omitted Abenaki County.

Contents ▲ ▲ ▲ ▲ ▲ ▲ ▲ ▲ ▲ ▲

Ladies and Gentlemen, the Show is about to commence.
You could not well expect to go in without paying,
but you may pay without going in.
I can say no fairer than that.

—Artemus Ward,
"At the Door of the Tent,"
Artemus Ward His Book

VACATIONLAND

1 ▲ ▲ ▲ ▲ ▲ ▲ ▲ ▲ ▲ ▲ ▲

In which we make the acquaintance of the genial showman and bringer of good cheer, Mr. Chick Devine, owner of the Chick Devine Fun O'Rama—and also meet the misguided youth, Roger Caron. The flight of the involuntary aerialist causes the Fun O'Rama to depart under cover of darkness for Abenaki County, the real Maine.

Now, AS IT HAPPENED, most of the trouble got started because Chick Devine lowered his standards. But in the old showman's defense, it was a rough summer down in Maine; the crowds were thin, there was plenty of rain, and as usual, help was hard to come by.

And it was just when it was hardest that the old Chicker let Roger Caron take the controls of the Flying Disc, which was just about the Fun O'Rama's biggest attraction.

The Disc was designed by Mr. Chick Devine himself and assembled by an old crony and hard-drinking mechanical engineer of his acquaintance.

It was a ride in which hearty souls were strapped onto a saucerlike object, hence the word *disc*, and then spun counterclockwise at high rates of speed while extremely loud music was played, greatly amplified to muffle the screams and pleadings of those fun-seekers who had been gullible enough to be enticed aboard.

The additional advantage of the Flying Disc, also an offspring of the fertile imagination of Chick Devine, was that the contents of passengers' pockets were frequently discharged in the course of their violent gyrations and landed underneath on a tarpaulin that had been erected for the purpose of collecting such valuables.

Money, watches, jewelry, wallets, handbags and such were then confiscated at the end of the day's merriment. False teeth, artificial limbs, funny hats, hearing aids, eyeglasses, footwear, canes, crutches, stuffed animals and other materials were dutifully turned over to the lost and found, operated by Mr. Chick Devine himself.

These items, whenever possible, were repatriated with their stunned and often weeping owners, many of whom vowed then and there to go no more a-roving on mechanical devices such as the Flying Disc.

Now, at the time which concerns us, the genial showman, Mr. Chick Devine, bringer of good cheer, prognosticator, pundit and promoter, had reached the age of three score. The venerable impresario, a son of the Pine Tree State, was then engaged in his life's work of operating the Chick Devine Fun O'Rama, "the greatest little big show Down East." On this particular occasion, the company had pitched camp among the citizens of Rockland, who were in a lather celebrating the Maine Seafood Festival, a week-long jubilee honoring the fruits of the sea and the culinary art of deep frying.

Being the professional bringer of family fun, as he called it, or fun for the whole family, Chick Devine maintained only the highest standards when it came to the recruitment of skilled personnel to aid him in bringing wholesome entertainment to the deserving citizens of Maine.

Unlike other such organizations of the carnival variety, Mr. Chick Devine's Fun O'Rama recruited only seasoned artistes and experienced technicians to operate the complex rides and other bits of amusement that made up his show. Failing that, the showman enlisted only fresh-faced youths, with a special preference given to ministerial candidates.

It was not Chick Devine's way to inquire of the local constabulary if there might be any idle corner boys about, any recently discharged young gentlemen from the House of Correction or persons of the traveling persuasion.

The best and the brightest served in the ranks of the Fun O'Rama and served there gallantly and with distinction.

"The lips that touch liquor will not tarry long near the controls of one of my amusement devices," the venerable Devine was oft heard to say while outlining his personal philosophy of family fun, "the Chick Devine code of family entertainment."

Across the state of Maine Mr. Chick Devine was known as a man who put the *vacation* in Vacationland and the *fun* in Fun O'Rama.

And so, when it was summer, Mainers thought of Chick Devine and the Fun O'Rama, for they knew he was coming.

In May, when there was still ice on the lakes and ponds upcountry, the first handbills and billboards began to appear, going up along the roadsides, plastered to telephone poles and barns. Verily there was not a town from Kittery to Calais in which a poster advising of the coming of the Fun O'Rama was not displayed.

Long before lilacs in the dooryard bloomed, the coming of Chick Devine blossomed from the side of silos and outbuildings, and it was impossible for any traveler to avoid the blessed news that the Fun O'Rama was once again en route.

The garish posters changed little over the years. They were still as cheaply printed as possible, featuring an arc of color and the words THE CHICK DEVINE FUN O'RAMA, and in smaller letters a partial listing of some of the upcoming show's highlights.

But always, every year, the posters carried the ageless likeness of the impresario himself, beaming benevolently on the state of Maine, one hand raised in the friendliest of waves.

"I have a duty to see to the quality of entertainment in this state. It's been my life's work. I know I've set my standards high, but people have come to expect that of me. They see the words *The Chick Devine Fun O'Rama*, and they know what to expect— they know their money's well spent and they know they're getting the kind of quality family fun that you just don't get much of these days," Chick Devine was telling a correspondent of the *Coastal Gazette* the night of Roger Caron's debut with the Flying Disc.

Roger was a misguided youth, friendless and alone in the cold world, until the old Chicker took pity on him and picked him up under somewhat unusual circumstances, but more of that anon.

Poor Roger had grown up at the New England Home for Little Wanderers, and he'd been wandering ever since the health-care professionals at that facility had given him his walking papers and bus fare. The sorry lad would have been heading straight for the license plate factory but for Chick Devine's heart of gold.

Perhaps the aging showman saw a bit of himself in the youth and thought of his own early years and his decision to make family fun his life's work after a bighearted jurist in his native Elm City gave him a choice of the open road or the Boys' Training Center.

On the evening in question young Roger had not entirely forsaken his tendencies toward the ways of sin and as a result had ingested strong drink and various pills. Alas, in the grip of these substances, the youthful entertainer and inexperienced technician had allowed the Flying Disc to reach a never-before-achieved rate of speed and as a result had fired one reveler—

who had inadvertently not been properly strapped in—across the show grounds, into the nearby business district and through a plate-glass window.

The involuntary aerialist, although not dead, had required extensive suture work and the ministrations of some of coastal Maine's finest surgeons. The subsequent publicity had nearly resulted in Roger's premature departure from the field of family entertainment and the temporary discontinuance of the Disc, pending the outcome of a thorough investigation by our staff of experts, as Chick Devine later told the local newspapers.

The incident weighed heavily on Chick's mind, so much so that for many months afterwards, he refused numerous pieces of registered mail from a law firm in Rockland.

As luck would have it, though, those celebrants attending the fryfest that evening were unaware that a mishap had taken place, believing that the flight of the involuntary aerialist across the heavens was just another of Chick Devine's efforts to bring quality entertainment to Maine.

A large crowd assembled following the aerial display, to inquire when the performance would be repeated and if there was an additional charge.

Despite the unfortunate launching, the kind of industrial mishap Chick Devine strove mightily to avoid, the showman appreciated spectacle wherever he found it. And so it was that he did not scold young Roger too long, preferring instead to accentuate the positive by complimenting the youth on his aim and the unscheduled display of airborne acrobatics to which the community had been treated.

Chick Devine mused on whether such a display might somehow be re-created on a regular basis and incorporated into the show, believing it would top any human-cannonball act in the Republic.

Fortunately for all concerned, the aerialist was made of sterner stuff, for a ride like that might have killed a lesser man, particularly with the plate-glass finale.

However, the genial showman was a much-experienced judge of matters calamitous and the repercussions that oft followed, and so it was that after returning from the hospital where he consoled the injured man's family, Chick Devine instructed his little band of merrymakers to pack their belongings and under cover of darkness slip off into the still of the night, bidding the rustics of Rockland adieu.

Chick Devine knew when to quit the field honorably and maintain the high standards for which he was known far and wide. He believed that legions of nay-sayers and the like were always lurking, waiting for an opportunity to besmirch his good name. To sully the honor of Devine. To trifle with him.

And he feared that the misfortune that had befallen his little band of players that evening would bring out what he called the very worst elements in our society, the lowest of the low, those who would seek to profit from calamity.

"Who's that?" asked Roger Caron as he helped Chick Devine pack.

"Lawyers. Or more specifically, that wicked cabal, the personal-injury lawyer. Oh, how his shadow has cast itself upon me before. As I said, I'll have none of this."

"And so we're leaving town?"

"I have instructed my professional colleagues to ready themselves for what we called the forced march in the old days of showmanship. We have pressing business elsewhere."

"Where are we heading, Mr. Chick?"

"Roger, we're going where small minds and greedy hearts won't be able to reach us. We're heading up-country, where men are still men, women are still women, and both parties are the better for it. We're heading where Maine is still Maine and where safety sob sisters and ambulance chasers can't reach us. We're going where the Flying Disc and you and I will be welcome and where fun for the whole family means just that—family fun. We're going where the family is still sacred and so is the fun."

"Is that in Maine?"

"Damn right it is. We're going to Abenaki County. You'll recall our previous outing among the Abenakians?"

"Yes, sir."

"Well, by God, you'll be back there soon enough, and you'll be glad of it. You'll be back down among God's own people. The real Mainers. None of these gentrified coastal dwellers and gawking tourists. No siree, Bob. We're heading back to the real Maine, and I can hardly wait to get there."

2 ▲ ▲ ▲ ▲ ▲ ▲ ▲ ▲ ▲ ▲

Whilst the showman and his ward motor toward their destination we insert certain information pertaining to Abenaki County for the edification of the reader.

ABENAKI COUNTY, Maine, boasts only one streetlight, and that is in Fillmore, the county seat. The streetlight has been broken for a number of years.

The shiretown is home to Abenaki State Teacher's College, now the University of Maine at Fillmore.

There are two mills in Fillmore. The first made shoes and the second made shirts, and neither any longer makes anything, for both are closed since those industries relocated to balmier climes in the nation's southland.

The lone remaining employer of Fillmoreans is the wood-turning plant, the Jewel Mills, which in its heyday claimed to be the largest producer of popsicle sticks, tongue depressors and toothpicks in the free world.

There is one state liquor store in Fillmore and four Baptist churches for Baptists of varying hues. Eight other Protestant denominations are also represented in the firmament, ranging from the Solid Rock Temple of New Jerusalem to the Unitarian Universalist Church much favored by collegians.

There is a Roman Catholic Church, the only representation of the Church of Rome in the county. If there are any Hebrews among the Abenakians, they have not made themselves known.

The county is, according to the most recent census figures available, ninety-seven percent of the Caucasian persuasion. The remaining three percent of Abenakians are presumed to be representatives of the region's "first citizens," Abenaki Indians who live on an abandoned stretch of railroad land known as "the tracks," near the county seat. It is the first place the local constabulary looks when any items are reported stolen.

A statewide effort at reorganizing and improving the Maine school system a number of years ago gave Abenakians a county-wide school administrative district, School Administrative District 13, or SAD 13, an abbreviation that has not gone entirely unnoticed.

About twenty percent of the county school system's graduates attend institutes of higher learning, and the vast majority of those matriculate at the local branch of the state university. More adventuresome souls, thirsty for knowledge, make the ninety-minute drive to Lewiston where a grander font bubbles.

There is also the Abenaki Vocational and Technical Institute, which is reputed to have the most extensive post–high school program in automotive sciences in the northeast—proof of which is abundant locally. There are some sixty licensed body shops in the county.

Abenaki County holds to a simpler code in these troubled and change-tossed times. Young women marry hereabouts and bring forth a new generation of Abenakians. Some bring forth a new generation without the benefit of the holy union.

The county has the highest rate of illegitimate births in Maine and for a number of years was often cited by national studies but now must rest on its laurels.

Abenaki County is bounded on the north by the Province

of Quebec, on the south by Kennebec County, to the west by Oxford and Androscoggin counties, and to the east by Somerset County.

The county is landlocked and is drained by the Slate River.

Each September, Fillmore plays host for one week to the Abenaki County Fair and Agricultural Exhibition, now in its 134th year. The fairgrounds is also the home of the harness horse racetrack. Amusements are hard to come by in the county. There are no movie theaters or bars. The Tri-County Raceway, where exhibitions of automotive prowess may be seen, is across the county line in Jay.

Early to bed is the wiser course of a Saturday night, but stalwarts insistent on a night of revelry have a few dance halls to choose from, most notably the Dozing Doe Lounge, which is open for business when not padlocked as a public nuisance.

During the year for which the most recent figures are available, more residents of Abenaki County were arrested for drunken driving and fish and game violations than in any other county in Maine.

The county seat is built around a modest square, which contains a bandstand and a roll of honor of fallen war dead who served with distinction in the Grand Army of the Republic and subsequent military assemblies.

On the east side of the square is the Abenaki County Court House, which is the home of the Abenaki County Court, presided over by the Honorable Rufus T. Spurgeon, a distinguished jurist.

Opposite the courthouse on the next corner is Red's Gas-N-Go, and next to this the Abenaki County Correctional Facility where penitents may be viewed, weather permitting, chopping wood or washing county police cruisers in the side yard as part of the rehabilitative process.

On the farther side of the square is the Farmer's Union; the

Chicken Coop, a twenty-four-hour eating establishment; and the beginnings of Fillmore's modest shopping district.

Beyond this is the college, and beyond the college are the agricultural showgrounds and the harness racetrack.

The Maine Central Railroad has discontinued service to the county. Two buses pass through town daily, the first heading to La Belle Province and the second en route from Quebec to points south. Travelers wishing to depart these environs may do so at these times. The bus service also provides the sheriff's office with a method for ridding the shiretown of drunkards, chronic mischief-makers, the occasional Abenaki Indian and other undesirables.

Although Maine is Vacationland, Abenaki County does not draw too many vacationers. The northern reaches of the county are, to the acre, owned by the Colburn Paper Company, which conducts an aggressive effort to discourage visitors.

The poetess Lillian McCrillis Sangerville, and Chester Greenwood, the inventor of the earmuff, are perhaps the county's most famous natives.

On the outskirts of Fillmore is Jerry's Liquidation City and Carpet Kingdom, owned and operated by State Representative Jerome B. Velure, a Republican. Nearby is the Greater Fillmore Industrial Park, unoccupied at this writing.

It should come as no surprise that Abenaki County is Maine's poorest—and that Chick Devine took his Fun O'Rama where it was most needed.

3 ▲ ▲ ▲ ▲ ▲ ▲ ▲ ▲ ▲ ▲

Ladies and gentlemen, presenting the Chick Devine Fun O'Rama, featuring melodious anthropoids, exotic fauna, medical curiosities, games of chance and exotic dancers. And much, much more.

PERHAPS A FEW WORDS on the composition of the Fun O'Rama are in order.

The acts changed over the years, year by year in most cases, and not infrequently, when artistic tempers flared, week by week. It was a show put together by Chick Devine during his annual winter sojourn in the Sunshine State, a period when he cased the residential hotels and trailer parks along the Gulf Coast which harbored the cream of the nation's second-string circuses and sideshows.

There in the fertile warmth of the Florida backwaters the cast of the next season's Fun O'Rama lay dormant, waiting to be summoned forth. And all that was necessary was for Chick Devine to cruise through his old haunts to gather together another season's band of merrymakers.

The rundown amusement parks and shabby animal farms like Gator Village and Chimpland that lined the old state highway that ran along the coast were ripe for the picking. Faithfully each year, these farm clubs sent Chick Devine his much-needed animal acts and curiosities.

Along these back roads it was possible to hire a quartet of chimpanzees who played a passable ragtime and wore red-and-white-striped blazers and straw boaters.

The sound of such an ensemble, wafting one quiet evening from a trailer, had piqued the prowling Chick Devine's curiosity and led to "Moe Havana and His Simian Sidemen," who hit the road for their first of many summers with the Fun O'Rama. The chimps worked Maine so many seasons in those days that Moe taught them a most spirited version of the Maine Stein Song—guaranteed to bring an audience to its feet.

There was something wonderful about sitting in the wooden bleachers in a town like Madawaska or Millinocket on a midsummer's eve and listening to the sound of those four melodious anthropoids as they worked their way through "If You Were the Only Girl in the World."

Along just such a highway Chick Devine had also stumbled across horses that could count, parrots who drank whiskey and spoke French—the exotic fauna that did little but burn hay but would draw a crowd in a place where no one had ever seen an armadillo or a pelican or a llama.

In a rundown hotel in East Naples, Chick Devine had discovered Pepe Baraja and his pups, Chi Chi, Lu Lu and Pepita.

And there were two other members of the Havana family, brothers Mel and Morty. Chick had run into the brothers at a dog track in central Florida where the pair were enjoying a bit of the sporting life. Over a few potables at a nearby roadhouse the brothers allowed that they had of late come into the possession of a moving van loaded with "medical curiosities" by way of a bankrupt medical school in the land of cotton.

And so it was that the brothers Havana joined the Fun

O'Rama with their wagonload of pathologists' souvenirs in formaldehyde.

But all of the talent that made up the Fun O'Rama was not imported from the nation's sunbelt, and some of Chick Devine's most important finds were made in the grand state of Maine, under often unexpected circumstances.

Such was the case of Francis Xavier Petroska, who was later to become Dr. Dynamite. Devine had picked up the good doctor at a moment when he was living in reduced circumstances. The man was a living relic from the golden days of itinerant demolition daredeviltry, who had made his name in the old blasting game by specializing in jobs that more cautious practitioners of the risky craft viewed as beyond them.

An unfortunate encounter with nitroglycerin while helping the good citizens of Cleveland forge ahead with urban renewal had sent Petroska to a veterans' hospital for an extended stay after a near stop at the pearly gates.

Now, at this point the Fun O'Rama also included several games of chance, including a shooting gallery designed to mystify even the steadiest of marksmen. There was in addition a maze through which a live mouse was enticed to rove while sportsmen stood about wagering on the rodent's destination. There was also an adults-only ring toss, a rather saucy enterprise featuring battery-operated booty as prizes, known in the trade as marital aids. This last endeavor, ever popular among the rustics, was the brainchild of Mr. Chick Devine. The prizes could only be obtained with a letter from a licensed physician, from an East Chicago mail-order house specializing in pharmaceutical and vulcanized items not customarily stocked at the neighborhood drugstore.

The show also featured an uncertain species of serpent, acquired from a Puerto Rican magician down on his luck at a jai alai fronton in Florida some years earlier. This creature was kept in a large steamer trunk into which ventilation holes had been drilled and on which the notice CAUTION: GIANT SNAKE had been stenciled.

The company at this time was rounded out, quite literally, by three young women of the exotic dancing sorority, Miss Cherry St. John, the star and owner of the Cherry St. John Chez Paree Revue, and her associates, Miss Jo Anne Flambé and Princess Sachem, the latter also known in the world of show business as the Native American Love Goddess. And, as Chick Devine was known to say, there was much, much more.

4 ▲ ▲ ▲ ▲ ▲ ▲ ▲ ▲ ▲ ▲

Chick Devine recalls his first encounter with young Roger. Hormarus Americanus, the scourge of Eggemoggin Reach, joins the Fun O'Rama.

Aɴᴅ sᴏ ᴛʜᴇ ɢᴇɴɪᴀʟ sʜᴏᴡᴍᴀɴ motored north toward Abenaki County at the wheel of his touring car whilst his young charge Roger slumbered fitfully in the backseat.

And Chick Devine recalled their fateful meeting of a few years earlier, which had come at the height of an artistic fracas.

The veteran impresario had been dealing with a mutiny in the ranks of his temperamental artistes at the time that had seen a number of the stars abscond with various properties owned by the Fun O'Rama because of a dispute over payment for services rendered.

Chick Devine was sitting in his trailer, contemplating the vagaries of family fun, when a knock at the door roused him from his musing. The handle of the trailer door turned very slowly, and the door opened to reveal a skinny, pale youth wearing a set of oily mechanics' coveralls. He was also soaking wet and sniffling and smiling nervously.

"Come in, come in, come in. And close the door for God's sake. That's right, drip water all over the place."

Chick knew the scenario that would follow, having heard such spiels a thousand or more times across most of the fifty states and Canada.

"Don't keep me in suspense. You want a job."

"I need a job," the young man said quietly.

"And you're a good worker, an honest worker," said Chick Devine.

"Yes . . ."

"I'll bet you don't drink, smoke, use drugs or associate with those that do," Chick continued.

"I don't. I don't."

"Well, well. You have no idea how rare those qualities are in a young man these days."

"Well?"

"Pity of it is, lad, but I'm not running the Moody Bible Institute here. Got that?"

The young man said nothing and stared back at Chick Devine. He saw a red-faced and slightly portly man of nearly sixty whose soft gray hair was cropped short. Chick Devine favored suits, preferably three-piece ones, with white shirts and ties a bit wider than the custom of the day. As he was in his office, he had his jacket off, sleeves rolled up. A cold cigar was held in his right hand.

"Listen, son. This is a carnival we've got here. You with me so far? Carnival. Comes from the old Latin expression meaning to say good-bye to meat. You with me so far?"

Chick Devine leaned forward and lit his cigar, drawing on it quickly.

"Well, I just said good-bye to more than meat. My meal ticket has run off. I got some serious problems here today. Am I going too fast for you?"

The young man continued to stare.

"At last count I'm down three strippers, a freak show and four musical monkeys. I'm not sure where Dr. Dynamite is, but that's about par for the course. All I've got to show for myself, my lad, is a nervous Mexican with three old dogs who can't remember half of their tricks. Hell, they'd be gone, too, but Pepe can't drive."

Chick Devine took a long pause and exhaled. The walls of his trailer were papered with dozens of framed newspaper clippings and photographs, and over his desk hung the state of Maine's flag.

"You still with me, pal? I am barely able to keep things afloat here. So you want a job? Sonny, I'm just about finished. So tell me, in twenty-five words or less, where you fit into this."

"Mr. Devine, I've got an act for your show."

"Sure you do. What're you, a country-western singer? Listen, let me tell you something. I don't book country-western singers. Nothing but trouble. Lost my last singing cowboy over in Frye-burg, morals charges."

"Look, please. Just come and see what I've got. It won't take five minutes," the young man pleaded.

"Listen, kid, I'll strangle you if I have to hear 'The Letter Edged in Black.'"

"Please."

"Don't whine. Look, how the hell did you get so wet? It's not raining that bad."

"I was having trouble with Ernie."

"Ernie?"

"Follow me and see."

Chick Devine hastened after the young man out of the trailer and over to a much-battered pickup truck with a wooden shed built onto the back. The young man opened the door of the shed, revealing a large, old-fashioned soft-drink machine, a kind of tank with a sliding top. He hopped up onto the back of the pickup and slid back the tank's top.

"Have a look," he beckoned to Chick Devine.

With some difficulty Chick Devine climbed up next to the youth. "Sweet jumping Jesus. Sweet jumping Jesus. Where in the name of the saints did you get that critter?"

The tank contained the largest lobster Chick Devine had ever seen.

"He's just shy of a hundred pounds, sir."

"Jesus H. Christ."

"Do you suppose folks would pay to have a look?"

"They might very well," said Chick Devine. "I've had stranger creatures in the show, but then again, I'd say this isn't bad. You know, in the old days a two-headed calf was about all you could hope for. God almighty, last year I had a guy round here with a kid in a cage, claiming the kid was an LSD victim. Kid just sat in the cage and drooled. Damn thing is we drew crowds that I'd have never expected."

According to Roger Caron, for that turned out to be the young man's name, the giant lobster had been found in the back of the pickup truck after the vehicle had been abandoned and towed to a gas station near Ellsworth where he worked. The owner of the gas station had given Roger the pickup truck and its passenger in lieu of back pay.

"Do you actually own this vehicle?" asked Chick Devine.

"He gave it to me."

"What about the title and registration?"

"I've got a license."

"That's swell. But the question is whether or not you legally own the truck and its contents. Follow me? You're driving a vehicle you don't own. Right? This rig could have been reported stolen or missing."

And so, after dark, Chick and Roger took the pickup truck out for a little spin and after first removing its license plates and making a few other alterations that Chick deemed necessary, they pushed it into a remote pond. The giant lobster remained back at the Fun O'Rama where its new career was about to start.

And so it came to pass that Roger and Ernie joined the Fun O'Rama and Chick Devine appointed Roger driver for Pepe and the pups.

Things began to pick up right away with the arrival of Roger Caron and his crustaceous ward. For one thing, the Fun O'Rama began getting some favorable publicity, much needed after some of its nasty scrapes on the road.

"Behind every cloud there's a silver lining, Roger. Ever hear that old chestnut?"

"I guess so, Chick."

"Well, I have always believed that behind every silver lining there's another cloud, usually bigger than the first. We must guard against this. You follow me?"

"Yes, sir."

"Grand. Well, as it happens, I have arranged a brief and not too exhaustive winter tour for your associate Ernest. Just a little something to keep the old boy in fighting trim until the sum-mer rolls around, you see. I took the liberty of booking the salt-water star into a few boat shows, couple of conventions, you know the kind of stuff I'm talking about. Look, this is found money, Roger. No sense letting somebody else make it. Am I right?"

"Yes, sir."

"Atta boy. You're a showman now."

An expert on marine life estimated the lobster to be at least two hundred years old, Chick Devine had begun to boast. Chick's expert was a general science teacher up at one of the regional high schools; still, he reasoned that the lobster had to be of an advanced age.

"And damn lucky to have avoided star billing at a clambake lo these many years, Roger," he advised the young man.

5 ▲ ▲ ▲ ▲ ▲ ▲ ▲ ▲ ▲ ▲

Marketing Maine-style, or how the impresario and his young ward presented the crustaceous behemoth to a curious public. A career is launched. A star is born. We first hear of the Crustacean Liberation Army.

THERE WAS NOT MUCH for the curious to do except file in and take a look at Ernie because all he did, whether on the road or back at the Fun O'Rama, was sit in his tank and sort of wiggle around a bit. Chick Devine had bought a larger tank, but otherwise that was it. No tricks. No actual performance. Just Ernie. One hundred pounds of Homarus Americanus.

"Homarus Americanus. How's that sound?"

"What is it?"

"That's Ernest's name in the language of the Caesars. I think it has a more powerful ring to it. Ernie is a bit too plebeian for my tastes."

The old Chicker got a tad carried away with himself and had taken an inordinate interest in the career of Ernie. Chick Devine's unusually fertile imagination had enjoyed a period of great fecundity and had run just a bit wild concocting the life story of Homarus Americanus.

Ernie's visitors, and they were many, particularly among tourists, winter and summer, were given a special pamphlet outlining the lobster's life story and the wild tale of his capture after a chase on the high seas during which the beast had rammed and sunk numerous pleasure craft and caused the loss of lives.

Chick Devine's poetic license had reached new levels as he detailed the three-day sea battle that was fought to capture the creature, "the scourge of Eggemoggin Reach," as he was also called.

The brochure showed a map of the chase area, complete with markings where vessels had been sunk and details of the number of hands lost when Ernie lurked in Maine's coastal waters.

Chick Devine had had the map of Ernie's bloody deeds at sea reproduced on thousands of paper placemats and distributed to diners and restaurants free of charge all along U.S. Route 1, the coast road.

The brochure also showed a slightly enlarged photograph of the lobster being loaded onto a flatbed railroad car by an enormous crane while thousands of ant-size onlookers gaped in horror.

An out-of-focus photograph bore the caption "At the Height of the Great Sea Battle," and purported to show U.S. and North Atlantic Treaty Organization naval vessels during the fierce fighting that went on before Ernie could be taken.

The actual photo had been taken during the battle of Jutland, but Chick Devine, while researching the production of the brochure, had taken a shine to it and clipped it out of the encyclopedia at the library.

Other photographs showed the terrified faces of military gunners manning shore installations along the Maine coast in anticipation of one of Ernie's rare, but nevertheless bloody, forays onto the mainland.

One photograph claimed to show National Guardsmen as-

sembled in Rockland to defend the city against Ernie's maraud-
ings. Another showed frightened refugees, their cars piled high
with mattresses and furniture, fleeing inland from small coastal
communities in anticipation of more shore leave for Ernie.

Wardens with helmets and flashlights were shown patrolling
the streets in other towns during the curfews that had been all
too common when Ernie roved the briny deep.

Chick Devine had dropped a few other photographs from his
presentation, including one that claimed to show Winston
Churchill, Joseph Stalin and Franklin Roosevelt meeting at Bar
Harbor to discuss what was to be done about Ernie. Chick sub-
stituted instead another photograph showing the Joint Chiefs
of Staff directing the search for Homarus Americanus.

The brochure and accompanying slide show that Fun O'Rama-
goers were treated to before they actually got in to see Ernie
was sufficient, in the words of Chick Devine, to make strong
men quake.

The walls of the tent were hung with old life rings from ships,
broken oars, masts and spars and other bits of marine debris
designed to create the impression of nautical nightmares.

Several complete skeletons were transferred over from the
brothers Havana's medical curiosities division. Ernie's tank was
ringed with barbed wire and signs in eleven languages warning
of danger.

Visitors were made to sign a legal-looking release that let
Chick Devine off the hook in case some unfortunate was
snapped up screaming and pulled back into the tank by the
crazed crustacean.

Pregnant women, small children unaccompanied by adults,
cardiac patients or anyone under a physician's care for nervous
disorders were cautioned to remain outside the exhibition.

And finally there was Roger Caron, resplendent in an old

deep-sea diving suit that Chick Devine had picked up in Wis-casset. Roger, who, viewers were told, was the only survivor of one of the vessels Ernie had sunk, stood next to the tank clutching a menacing-looking spear gun and occasionally gave the lethargic Ernie a few prods with an old boat hook when the terrified visitors seemed disappointed by his docile demeanor.

Chick Devine often added to the festivities by donning oil-skins and carrying a submachine gun under one arm and a be-laying pin in his other hand while he cautioned the curious against getting too close to the tank.

The entire presentation was usually narrated by Chick him-self, with the assistance of a large number of sound effects: heav-ily amplified splashing sounds; waves crashing on rocks; and gale-force winds, actually the sound track from an old film of a typhoon ravaging the island of Borneo.

The entire presentation was also on tape in the event that Chick's ministrations down at the Swedish ring toss kept him occupied.

And so it was, all in all, that the career of the fabled crusta-cean was a resounding success in the Pine Tree State and points farther afield.

A restaurant in New York City offered a large sum for Ernie, promising merely to exhibit him in a tank to wow jaded urban diners. But, in spite of the sum, Chick Devine remained true to his word and kept Ernie and Roger on at the Fun O'Rama.

And then one morning, just while all was going fine and dandy, Roger found a strange letter under the door of his trailer.

"They want Ernie," he told Chick Devine.

"They all want Ernie," Chick replied, not bothering to look up. The bringer of family fun was deep in thought as he perused the morning line on a number of thoroughbreds and drank his coffee.

"He's a star, Roger. The biggest lobster in the Christian world. Why, last night alone more than three hundred devotees filed in to pay their fifty cents to see the fabled Ernie, the scourge of Eggemoggin Reach."

"But they want us to free him," said Roger.

"Free? Free? Nothing is free in this life, my lad. Nothing. And Ernie is one of life's bargains, a mere fifty centavos. Half a buck. Four bits. A pittance. A drop in the old bucket. A spit in the ocean. Hell, there's not much you can get these days for fifty cents. But we make an exception to that. For fifty cents you can see this mighty denizen of the Gulf of Maine, a bit of living history as it were."

"You don't understand, Chick. Someone wants to free Ernie. They want him back in the ocean."

"Free Ernie?" Chick Devine repeated. "Why, we can't free Ernie. We can't free Ernie any more than we could eat him. Lord almighty, he's worth his weight in gold. Let me tell you this, pal. He's worth three LSD victims by my reckoning."

"But they said we had to do it or they'd rescue him."

"What in God's name are you talking about?"

The note read as follows.

To Whom It May Concern:
Chick Devine's Fun O'Rama is exploiting and abusing a harmless creature and misleading thousands of innocent people in its presentation of "Homarus Americanus, the scourge of Eggemoggin Reach." It is false and misleading to claim that the hundred-pound lobster you have imprisoned knew George Washington, is a danger to bathers along the Maine coast, a hazard to navigation and was captured only after a sea battle in which many lives were lost. We know your presentation to be full of lies and exaggerations. There is no proof of a lobster crawling out

of Penobscot Bay on to U.S. Route 1 and grabbing onto a carload of tourists before returning to the sea. You have twenty-four hours to free this harmless creature or face the consequences.

The Crustacean Liberation Army

"Well, I'll be dipped," said Chick Devine.

6 ▲ ▲ ▲ ▲ ▲ ▲ ▲ ▲ ▲ ▲

In which we learn of the abduction of Homarus Americanus by certain crustaceous liberators and what came of all of this.

THERE WERE ONLY TWO active members of the Crustacean Liberation Army, the poet and outdoorsman Vance Lancet and his associate, Cliff Leach, an organic farmer and radio talk-show host. But these two, misguided as they were, toppled an empire, to use a phrase employed by Chick Devine himself.

For it was Lancet and Leach who were responsible for the abduction and tragic, although accidental, death of the fabled crustacean Ernie, also known as Homarus Americanus, the scourge of Eggemoggin Reach, and so forth.

Later, at their trial, Leach and Lancet threw themselves on the mercy of the special fish and game tribunal, and in the end, the State of Maine agreed to ask for leniency in sentencing if the pair of misguided liberators of crustaceans would make a full confession.

Chick Devine and Roger Caron urged the special prosecutor to show no quarter and hoped that Leach and Lancet would receive the most severe of punishments.

Realizing they were in hotter water than anything Ernie had

ever confronted, Vance and Cliff obtained the services of one of Maine's most brilliant advocates, Harrison Janney III, a senior partner in the fine old Portland firm of Janney, Miles and Leeds, who was widely known for his many unsuccessful attempts to become Maine's governor.

Serving in the capacity of special prosecutor was the fabled jurist Holbrook Currier, many years before the bar and personal attorney for Chick Devine and his various enterprises.

The trial, which pitted these two legal campaigners against each other, drew enormous crowds, including many hundreds of law students who were bused in from far and wide as well as representatives of the wholesale seafood industry. The turnout and extensive pretrial publicity resulted in moving the trial to an ice hockey arena outside Madawaska in the northern reaches of the state where it was hoped that an impartial jury could be found.

The entire proceedings were broadcast live on the public radio and television network as the eyes and ears of Maine remained fixed to their televisions and radios. School was canceled, vacations taken and in some sections the economy ground to a standstill.

In his opening remarks Holbrook Currier painted Leach and Lancet as desperate men who had been unable to intimidate the operators of the Fun O'Rama and, to use their words, "vicious exploiters of this simple creature of the deep." And so they took the law into their own hands.

And one dark night, when all was quiet at the Fun O'Rama and Chick Devine and Roger were snoozing, Leach and Lancet, dressed completely in black, their faces smudged with burnt cork, had staged a daring commando raid on the exhibition where Ernie was incarcerated against his will, or so they maintained.

As fate would have it, neither Cliff nor Vance were physically up to snuff when it came to lugging a soaking-wet hundred-pound lobster any distance, particularly when the crustacean in question was resisting this attempt to free him.

Both Cliff and Vance abhorred firearms and violence, but feeling that the moment required some accessories, they brought along a box of railroad flares.

The original plan for the middle-of-the-night maneuver to spring Ernie called for him to be taken immediately to the Church of the Goodsportsman for sanctuary. However, Father Romeo Bissonette's interpretation of canon law was along such lines that the curate did not view Ernie as a suitable candidate for such protection.

So, after a heated wrestling match with Ernie, during which both Cliff and Vance received more than a few painful pinches from the very creature they were trying to aid, the two Crustacean Liberation Army commandos were able to drag the ungrateful lobster a short distance and load him into the backseat of Vance's car.

And off into the dark night they went.

With Vance at the wheel and Cliff in the backseat, still struggling and attempting to restrain the thrashing Ernie, the pair motored toward the coast where they planned to reunite Ernie with his kith and kin at high tide.

Despite being out of his natural habitat at this late hour, and holding a serious weight disadvantage as Cliff Leach easily weighed seventy pounds more, Ernie put up a furious fight. The screams of Cliff Leach as he attempted to place a full nelson on the slippery Ernie could be heard as Vance roared through the night, heading coastward.

But with Cliff and Ernie locked in wild combat in the backseat of the speeding getaway car, the poet Vance Lancet, unfamiliar with the rural byways of Maine, was having a deuce of a time at the wheel.

It is not any easy thing to drive a car in the dead of night on the narrow and twisting side roads of Maine when a wrestling match of some magnitude between a man and a hundred-pound lobster is raging in the backseat of one's car.

And so the poet Vance Lancet, nervous as only the makers of poesy can be, was making a holy show of the drive, weaving wildly from one lane to another and alternately accelerating and braking suddenly. Several times during the drive Ernie's tail flicked out to give Vance a sound box behind the ear on his right side, further interfering with the driver's concentration.

Halfway to the coast, the hostilities in the rear of the getaway car in full gear, the poet Vance Lancet took his eyes off the road momentarily to glance over his shoulder and was startled to see that the crustaceous crusher now had a firm headlock on Cliff Leach, who was screaming for reinforcements.

Alas, before the poet could slow down and come to a stop to assist his fellow commando, he lost what little control he still had, and the car, with Vance, Cliff and the belligerent Ernie aboard, went flying off the road and crashed into the side of the Full Gospel Tabernacle in Alna.

The sound of this late-night collision roused the citizenry in that peaceful locale and brought a number of curiosity seekers as well as officials to the scene of the mishap.

As many of the bystanders would later testify, the crash had badly damaged the vehicle, pinning Vance and Cliff inside and throwing Ernie, the other midnight rider, out through a rear window.

Although Vance and Cliff did not require immediate medical attention, once they were freed from their confines, both complaining of bruises and badly shaken, this was not the case with Ernie.

The crash had tossed him through the air some distance, leaving him unconscious on the ground. Members of the volunteer rescue squad in Alna, who assembled to view the carnage, were unsure of how to deal with this unusual accident victim.

But quick thinking prevailed and Ernie was loaded, with some difficulty, aboard the ambulance for the ride to the hospital in Bath.

Halfway there, with Ernie's vital signs failing, the ambulance crew decided to detour to a nearby lobster pound where they hoped experts would be more able to cope with such a crisis. But this was not to be. And Ernie was, in the words of his obituary in the *Abenaki Clarion*, "called to glory" shortly before the ambulance could reach the pound.

At the trial both Leach and Lancet were sobbing uncontrollably when the ambulance attendants testified about Ernie's last moments among the living. Roger Caron was badly shaken by the whole experience, as was the usually stoic Chick Devine, who was observed to sniffle.

At this point in the hearing into the well-intentioned but errant crustacean liberators' actions, Holbrook Currier introduced a series of newspaper clippings dealing with the abduction and death of Ernie, including a special investigative piece in the *Sunday Telegraph* entitled "A Lobster Called Ernie," which went on to win many prizes at the Maine Press Association festival later in the year.

As it turned out, Cliff Leach and the poet Vance Lancet were saved by Harrison Janney III's brilliant legal maneuvering and plea bargaining, along with an uncharacteristic display of mercy by Judge Rufus T. Spurgeon.

In what was to become known as "the shore dinner defense," Janney successfully argued that his clients were not acting from selfish motives but really believed, however misguided, that they had Ernie's welfare and best interests at heart.

They only wished to return the pugnacious critter to his natural home. His death was purely accidental.

Janney called a number of experts as well as character witnesses who testified to the upstandingness of Cliff and Vance and reported that both men had been required, because of the horrible trauma of the accident and the death of Ernie, to undergo special counseling every week from Maeve Rideout, a licensed paracrustaceous psychologist, a rare science that explores the relationship between man and crustaceans.

Ms. Rideout told the court that the poet Vance Lancet was taking the tragedy particularly hard and had required sedation en route to the trial after stopping at a diner in Mars Hill where the waitress had placed a paper placemat in front of him showing how to eat a lobster.

In an extraordinary display of both sensitivity and judicial widsom, Judge Spurgeon ordered both Cliff Leach and Vance Lancet to perform one thousand hours of community service by taking underprivileged youngsters to visit crustaceans and also by taking crustaceans and mollusks to visit shut-ins, a form of therapy recommended by Ms. Rideout.

An interdenominational memorial service was later held for the fallen crustacean, jointly presided over by the Reverend Dr. Don Olay of the Solid Rock Temple of the New Jerusalem, and Father Romeo Bissonette, who had had some second thoughts about failing to offer sanctuary to the deceased.

The Havana brothers' musical charges played "Over the Waves"; a selection of the poems of Lillian McCrillis Sangerville were read by her great niece, Charmaine McCrillis Dinsmore, including the popular, "God Speed Thee, Little Lobster"; and, as he was known to do, Mr. Chick Devine had a few words to say.

7 ▲ ▲ ▲ ▲ ▲ ▲ ▲ ▲ ▲ ▲

A remembrance of mutinies past, including the misbehavior of the Native American Love Goddess and the midnight ride of Victor Fontaine.

ALTHOUGH THE TRAGEDY of Homarus Americanus was one of the greatest with which Mr. Chick Devine was forced to deal, his life in the world of family fun was fraught with quandaries.

Just prior to the arrival of young Roger and his crustaceous companion, the impresario had been embroiled in knotty personnel matters.

A week of heavy rain had dampened the spirits of Chick's little gang of fun-makers, and they were now, as is so often the case with those of artistic temperament, making demands.

These particular demands involved payment for services rendered to the Fun O'Rama. Several of the artistes, including such veteran ingrates as the Havana brothers, wanted to see some good-faith gas money up front, at least enough to get them and their rolling collection of medical curiosities and musical monkeys off to a fresh start.

The lovely and talented Miss Cherry St. John and her two lithesome associates were also in the ranks of the mutineers on this occasion and were eager to take the Chez Paree Revue where its refinements would be more appreciated.

And lest we forget, among the mutineers on that occasion, the usually faithful Pepe Baraja, who should have known better after his many seasons on the road with Chick Devine. A skilled handler of the canine species, Pepe and his Pups were a veritable fixture with the Fun O'Rama. Alas, a rough and rainy season in Maine had the even loyal Pepe longing for his native Nogales.

And so it was that once again the patience of the old showman was being tested in his struggle to bring quality entertainment to the culture-starved Yankees.

As it happened, the normally loquacious Devine found himself at a loss for words and losing control of the polemics.

The brothers Havana—Moe, Mel and Morty—never any good at dealing with stress, were shouting about getting the sheriff down to the Fun O'Rama. Cherry St. John, for some odd reason, was weeping uncontrollably.

And to add to the confusion raging inside Devine's tiny trailer, the equally excitable Señor Baraja had brought along the pups, Lu Lu, Chi Chi and Pepita, and those furry stars were doing their level best to further the disruption.

"This is it, Chick," said Mel Havana.

"This is definitely it, Chick," said Moe Havana.

"Boys, boys," pleaded Chick Devine. "Please, let's try to be reasonable. Let's try to have dialogue. Like businessmen. Like entertainers. A little of the old give-and-take, please."

"We've had a little of the old give-and-take already from you, Mr. Chick Devine," said Mel Havana.

"We give, you take," said brother Morty.

"We don't want dialogue. We want travelogue. We want our money," said Mel.

"A fine situation after all these years. You're biting the very hand that has fed you. The very shoulder you have leaned on.

Your old pal, Chick Devine," said Chick.

"We don't want any more pine trees. We want palm trees. Florida, here we come," said Morty.

"Morton, Melvin, Morris. This is breaking an old man's heart. Is this the way you're leaving?" asked Chick.

"No, we aren't going until we get some simoleons out of you," said Mel.

"Look, boys, this is all so sudden. And you fellas know what the gate's been like. Boys, it's been raining cats and dogs. The good people of Maine are staying home."

"That's where we're going. Home," said Moe.

"I've got to have a few days to reassess the cash flow," said Chick Devine.

"No tricks, Chickie. Don't forget, we know you from way back," said Morty.

"Morton," said Chick Devine with great indignation.

"Don't Morton me. Get our money."

"My heart is breaking," said Chick Devine.

"Let's get out of here," said Mel Havana, and the brothers trooped out of Chick's trailer.

"This is a sad day, indeed," said Chick Devine, looking at the departing Havana brothers. "And it looks like it might get sadder," he added.

"Chick, enough is enough," said Cherry St. John. "This has been the worst season in years—and the last two weeks, what with the rain and the problems in Caribou. We just can't go on."

The problems in Caribou are your problems, sweetheart, Chick Devine was thinking to himself. *I wash my hands of that whole deal.*

An incident that had taken place in Caribou, costing the Fun O'Rama a thousand dollars and some embarrassing publicity, was in part responsible for that afternoon's confrontation.

Princess Sachem, the Native American Love Goddess, also

known as Angela Mannucci, had gotten herself and, by association, the entire ensemble, in difficulties with the authorities in the land of the potato blossom.

An ingenue that season, fresh off the farm in Union City, New Jersey, Miss Mannucci, or Princess Sachem, had been charged with the performance of a lewd dance by narrow minds in that Aroostook County community.

Both Chick and Cherry had scolded the girls in the past about allowing their creative urges to get the better of them, but the roar of the greasepaint proved too much for the histrionic princess on the fateful evening in question.

And so it was, midway through her solo, a traditional fertility dance in which she was joined by the Fun O'Rama's faithful reptilian companion, that the long arm of the law snatched her off the stage and off to the local jail.

Chick Devine had been down on the midway at the time, operating the ever-popular Swedish ring toss of which we have previously spoken.

And Cherry was back at her trailer, primping for her grand finale when the princess ran afoul of the law.

Unfortunately the arresting officers were in plain clothes as part of their effort to spy on the Fun O'Rama's frivolities, and the princess, suspecting some carnal irregularities as the officers climbed on stage, dispatched the first lawman with a haymaker of the old school. It was only after what the local newspaper later characterized as a "ferocious affray" that the dancing pugilist was hauled off.

So it was that Chick Devine was required to make a guest appearance down at the city jail in the hopes of obtaining the release of the princess.

It was not Chick Devine's first visit to the local hoosegow in Caribou, for during a previous swing through northern Maine a few years back, he had had other cause to tarry at the police station.

At that time his presence was required at the lockup when Victor Fontaine, a son of Abenaki County who was working that season at the Fun O'Rama as an aide-de-camp, had gone astray.

Victor had, in the words of the desk sergeant, unlawfully used a motor vehicle without the owner's permission. This bit of mischief had taken place at a rather late hour after Victor and several of his play fellows from the Fun O'Rama had quaffed a number of potations made from grain alcohol. Victor's usually good judgment and decorous comportment were further enkindled by the ingestion of several capsules given to him by a stable hand who said they would make an old horse feel young again.

Thus fortified, Victor sallied off to the Big Pine Motor Mart near the fairgrounds and test-drove a spanking new pickup truck.

Although it was three A.M., Victor had not yet aroused the suspicions of the local authorities as the only constable on duty, Patrolman Arnold Togue, was bracing himself against the night air with a hot cup of coffee at the Big Rig Plaza, an all-night diner much popular with long-distance truckers and potato pickers.

Victor was not to be so easily ignored, so he made several passes through the center of slumbering Caribou with his hand on the pickup's horn and the radio blaring. For good measure Victor fired off a number of rounds from a starter pistol he'd found earlier back at the Fun O'Rama.

Victor then drove across a dozen front lawns and clipped a couple of headstones in a family burial plot. In no time he had the attention he was seeking, and Patrolman Togue was in hot pursuit.

The intemperate Victor then led the patrolman on a wild chase around the community during which an even more considerable amount of damage was done, primarily by the patrol car operated by the constable. Togue lacked experience in conducting high-speed chases, but he more than made up for this with his enthusiasm. The results produced an insurance adjuster's field day as Victor and the patrolman careened through Caribou, sideswiping parked cars and clipping fire hydrants.

The demolition derby then moved away from the town center out along the main road where Victor led his pursuer through several gardens and across an athletic field.

Victor and the pickup parted company after it became bogged down in a ditch, and the chase continued on foot with Patrolman Togue bringing up the rear. The finale of Victor's late-night ride ended in a frantic dash across an open field in the dark. The excesses of the evening were beginning to wear Victor down, and in the dark he staggered across what turned out to be a recently abandoned septic tank.

Patrolman Togue, close on Victor's heels, also followed along, and both of them found themselves awash in a most unpleasant predicament.

It was a full forty-five minutes before the relief column located the pair still paddling about in the vat of night soil. Long ladders were called for, and after a few more minutes' delay, Victor and the patrolman malodorously rose from the tank.

Despite their condition, neither appeared to require the immediate services of a physician, and although they failed to appreciate the situation, their condition was the cause of more than a little mirth among the company of rescuers, which included a number of nearby residents, several members of the volunteer fire company and quite a few curiosity seekers from the Big Rig Plaza.

After assessing the situation the members of the rescue party unanimously agreed that placing Victor and the pungent patrolman in the squad cars was out of the question, given the state of their persons. And so the unlawfully used pickup truck was freed from the ditch, and both of the nocturnal swimmers were returned to town, riding in the rear of the vehicle.

Although the hour was late, a loud and waggish crowd of enthusiasts assembled outside the police station to greet the fragrant duo, and their embarrassment was lengthened when the desk sergeant insisted that both men be hosed off in the parking lot next to the jail.

Several hours after this Chick Devine was roused from his slumber to appear at the jail on behalf of the misguided Victor.

As the rest of his little troupe was still deep in sleep, Chick decided that he would have to make the trip into town alone to deal with the authorities.

At the jail Chick found Patrolman Togue bemoaning the loss of his new uniform and worrying whether his service revolver would ever return to the line of duty after its dip. The desk sergeant, a meticulous man much fond of paperwork, was coaching Patrolman Togue in the composition of his report. He was also, with the aid of an adding machine, attempting to estimate the amount of damages resulting from the chase.

At least sixteen citizens had already reported their vehicles victims of the chase, and the director of public works was still out cruising the side streets seeing how many signs, fire hydrants and utility poles had been wounded in the fray.

Victor was feeling the effects of his revels and was sitting on the floor of the holding cell with his head hung over the edge of the commode. His own clothing had been seized for sanitary reasons, and he was wrapped in a blanket.

"How's it going, Vic," said Chick Devine.

"I'm dying. I'm dying," moaned Victor.

"Guess you had a little problem last night," said Chick Devine.

Victor did not look up again and said nothing, so after a few minutes of listening to him moan, Chick left the former Fun O'Rama fun-maker to his suffering and returned to the front desk.

Although Chick Devine hated to see a fellow showman in a jam, there were limits. And Chick Devine was sure that Victor's midnight ride was going to cost somebody or other plenty. So he was weighing how to best disassociate himself from Victor's revels.

Back at the front desk the sergeant was cheerfully tallying the damages, which had now moved into six figures.

"How's your pal?" the sergeant asked.

"I wouldn't call him my pal," said Chick Devine.

"Well, he works out there at your show, doesn't he?"

"He may. I don't recognize him, really. There are so many of these guys. They come and go."

"I suppose they do," said the sergeant.

"Well, I don't know what to say," said Chick Devine. "I'll stop back later to see how he's feeling."

"Fine."

But Chick Devine had not come back to see Victor Fontaine. The Fun O'Rama had only one day left in potato country, and so, with a three-week stint in the Maritime Provinces coming up, Chick Devine decided that the midnight ride of Victor Fontaine might be too much for his enterprise to sustain. And so he ordered all hands to break camp.

It was not necessary to break the news to the company; such things travel fast in the world of family entertainment. The events had also been reported on the local radio station where the announcer had taken to referring to Victor as "a drug-crazed carnival roustabout."

Chick Devine was leading the Fun O'Rama across the border into New Brunswick the last time he heard a radio news report on his former employee.

8 ▲ ▲ ▲ ▲ ▲ ▲ ▲ ▲ ▲ ▲

How the poet and outdoorsman Vance Lancet came to dwell in the Pine Tree State. The meeting of the poet and Cliff Leach, which led to their co-hosting The Garden of the Airwaves, *in which agronomy is made simple.*

As it happened the poet and outdoorsman Vance Lancet came to Maine in search of the good life by way of a writer's workshop held each summer on Cape Squab at the artists' retreat Pomona.

One taste of Maine was enough for the lyrical Lancet, who abandoned the evils of city living to dwell on an unpaved back road a few miles outside of Fillmore in a ramshackle cabin that an earlier and less hearty sod-buster had erected in his quest for the good life.

The builder of this demesne had felt a sudden urge to travel south the second time his pipes froze, leaving the property in some disrepair and a burden to the already overburdened tax rolls in Abenaki County.

Unable to find a suitable buyer locally, the selectmen in Fillmore had engaged the services of State Representative Jerome B. "Jerry" Velure, the Abenaki County Republican and owner of Jerry's Liquidation City and Carpet Kingdom, to find a suitable candidate for this remote dream house.

An ad in an environmental newspaper in New York City had netted some three thousand serious inquiries, further complicating the process, but only the poet Vance Lancet had actually driven up to view the property. He arrived one fine day in a battered foreign car, the first such vehicle seen in the area, and Jerry Velure decided that he would not let Vance get away.

Vance impressed the selectmen and Jerry Velure right from the start as just the right man for the property. He wanted to live in rural Maine more than anything else in the whole world, and he had none of the skills necessary to do that. But he did have sufficient funds to purchase the "secluded woodland retreat" that he had read of in far-off New York City.

"The perfect candidate," Jerry Velure told the selectmen.

And so Buster and Junior Flagg, selectmen and operators of the Star Route truck that hauled the mail from Fillmore to the Canadian line and back again each day, and Luther Finch, retired manager of the Farmer's Union, along with Jerry Velure, bundled Vance into a four-wheel-drive and motored out to view nature's wonders and the less spectacular works of man at the abandoned homestead.

Vance was telling the others how much peace and quiet meant to him, and so he was delighted when he saw that the road was not paved.

"No neighbors for a good three miles," said Buster Flagg.

"Delightfully private," said Jerry Velure.

"Wonderful," said Vance.

Although Jerry Velure had been prepared, should the situation arise, to hard-sell the property, this was one of those cases where the place just sold itself.

Vance had already made his decision on the drive up from New York, repeating the real estate notice over and over in his head. He was now like a man in a trance, standing on the half-finished deck in front of the cabin, breathing deeply.

Buster and Junior Flagg shifted uneasily from one foot to the other as they eyed the secluded woodland retreat. A few sheets of plastic, which had been nailed over the windows several winters past, were flapping in the breeze. The cabin, even on that mild morning, looked sorrier than it had the last time Jerry Velure and the selectmen had hauled a prospective good-life seeker up the narrow, rutted road to see it.

Fortunately there had not been much rain and the road was passable.

The Flagg brothers let Jerry Velure do most of the talking, and Luther Finch, whose hearing aid was down in Portland for an overhaul, just smiled.

The previous owner, who had planned to open a bookstore and natural food restaurant here, had left the property in a state known to real estate agents and other professional optimists as "the handyman's special."

A goodly number of building supplies had been abandoned around the property, including stacks of cinder blocks, sacks of cement, pipes, lumber and tools. A couple of Maine winters had made most of these items appear much older than they actually were.

There was a kind of pen out in the back, now overgrown with scrub, where the previous pilgrim had kept a couple of goats which he had planned to launch into the cheese business. The goats had other plans and departed for points unknown.

There were also the remains of an old truck that had apparently been used to haul supplies up to the cabin and was now mired on the roadside, its windows shot out by passing marksmen who had overlooked the prominent NO HUNTING signs posted along the road.

"This is one of the quietest places in northwestern Maine," said Junior Flagg, eager to seem part of the sales process.

You could be dead out here for three or four weeks, nobody would miss you, thought Buster Flagg.

But Vance just stood on the porch, breathing deeply with his eyes half open and fingering some little wooden beads that he'd been nervously playing with during the drive up.

"You a Catholic?" asked Luther Finch.

"What?" said Vance. "Oh, no, these are my worry beads."

"Well, you won't need them anymore, young fella," said Buster Flagg. "You can leave your worries behind you. Nothing to worry about up here."

"The air is wonderful," said Vance.

"It's free too," said Junior.

Jerry Velure cleared his throat and smiled a bit nervously.

"When could I move in?" Vance asked.

"Move in," the Flagg brothers said in unison.

"Tomorrow. Why, right now. Whenever you'd like," said Jerry Velure.

"You really want to buy this place?" asked Buster.

Jerry Velure stared coolly at Buster.

"Sure, but what about all the paperwork and the settlement?" asked Vance.

"Don't worry about things like that. This is Maine. A man is as good as his handshake. Why, we'll have you installed up here in short order," said Jerry Velure.

"Great," said Vance.

"Let's shake on it," said Jerry Velure.

The Flagg brothers, fearful of saying the wrong thing, were walking back toward the four-wheel-drive with Luther Finch.

"Jesus, he's going to buy this place," said Buster.

"Never even asked about the price," said Junior.

And so it was that the selectmen and Jerry Velure installed Vance Lancet, poet and property owner, at the end of that long, unpaved road, far from the madding crowd and everything else.

He learned later about the shallow well and the broken septic system and what happened to his long, unpaved driveway in the spring.

But the poet Vance Lancet was never heard to complain about these inconveniences, believing as he did that such things were part of the good life.

He just moved up there and put up more NO HUNTING signs and hunkered down and stuck it out. He called the place the Glade, and put a sign down on State Route 27 advising passersby of his whereabouts.

His new quarters did not, strickly speaking, resemble a glade as one thinks of a glade, but then, up in Maine, one man's glade is another man's shallow well.

The selectmen, unlike Jerry Velure, experienced some remorse for their part in the property transaction and conditions up at the Glade, and Buster and Junior took to stopping in from time to time, when they could get up the road, to see how the poet was faring.

And so it was that Vance Lancet came to live in the Glade and people got used to seeing him around Fillmore with his knapsack hung over his shoulder. Vance had opinions on all subjects, and people in the county seat enjoyed talking to him because he always had plenty of time to talk, for he had nothing else to do.

During the long winter nights up in the Glade, snowbound and itchy with cabin fever, Vance had taken to calling up a popular local radio talk show, *The Garden of the Airwaves*, hosted by Cliff Leach, an organic farmer and hermit. In no time at all the poet and the radio talk-show host were fast friends.

Both Vance and Cliff were graduates of the Pomona summer seminar.

Vance was a great fan of *The Garden of the Airwaves*, particularly a weekly feature Cliff did on dealing with unwanted insects in the home or garden, called "Pests Aside."

On "Pests Aside," Cliff told amusing real-life stories about house and garden pests he had known, or he read anecdotes about pesky garden visitors sent in by his many avid listeners, who tuned in weekly to hear about the merry doings in Cliff's garden.

Cliff also included poems and the occasional song in his repertoire of herbal humor. Vance never missed a show, taping them frequently to play back.

He particularly enjoyed "Ask Cliff," the portion of the program in which the horticulturist of the airwaves freely dispensed gardening advice to his listeners. Each week, in every season, Cliff instructed those eager to till the ground.

At first Vance was only a frequent caller, but soon, after a meeting between the two naturalists, Cliff and Vance became co-hosts.

Now, some may wonder as to the results of diagnosing plant ailments over the telephone and then dispensing free advice and prescribing treatment for the ailing flora. The results were quite mixed. And Cliff and Vance were often the recipients of large volumes of mail from elderly listeners whose much beloved houseplants and even the occasional cat had taken a turn for the worse after a hearty dose of a radio remedy.

Sometimes these well-intentioned but distraught individuals took to calling *The Garden of the Airwaves* during the live broadcast portion of the program and caused a disruption by threatening, weeping or otherwise drawing attention to themselves, and embarrassing Cliff and Vance before the audience at home.

There was even an item in one of the Portland papers during the winter after the pair prescribed a special potion guaranteed to prolong the life and vitality of the popular Christmas poinsettia. Readers were warned by an agronomist at the University of Maine not to dose their plants with the radio-recommended potion as it would bring about their immediate demise.

But despite the frequent critical phone calls and volume of unflattering mail, Cliff and Vance persisted in bringing this special information to the airwaves each week.

State Representative Jerry Velure, who also owned WEZY AM-FM, the voice of Abenaki County, was a champion of freedom of information and also most pleased that *The Garden of the Airwaves*, which the solon had his doubts about, was being sponsored by the Garden of Eden, a natural foods store and café in the county seat. It was not easy to find sponsors for programs very early on a Sunday morning unless they were involved with spreading the good word of the risen Christ.

So although Jerry Velure, and apparently an ever-growing number of listeners, had serious doubts about the gardening acumen of Cliff and Vance, the show, as they say, went on.

Jerry Velure reasoned that most Abenakians were abed at that unwholesome hour and the rest were too smart to take such advice, especially from a couple of out-of-staters.

Cliff and Vance, being otherwise without visible means of support, spent the remainder of their days fighting the good fight in any number of causes and such.

Most days, weather permitting, and often when the weather did not permit, they had a table set up in front of the Farmer's Union, or the Chicken Coop, or Red's Gas-N-Go, as they solicited signatures for petitions, passed out leaflets and asked for contributions.

Theirs were lives dedicated to saving the whale, braking for animals, getting Uncle Sam's hands off Central America and splitting wood, not atoms.

9 ▲ ▲ ▲ ▲ ▲ ▲ ▲ ▲ ▲ ▲

Two old showmen are reunited. We learn of the legacy of the poetess Lillian McCrillis Sangerville. And Chick and the professor take tea at Forsythia Lodge, where the grand historical pageant is outlined.

Iɴ ᴛʜᴇ ᴘᴇᴀᴄᴇꜰᴜʟ, if remote, Abenaki County seat there dwelt one Lee Berlitz, an old confidant of Chick Devine's and playmate from earlier days when both gentlemen had labored in the fields of family fun.

The two showmen had spent many the pleasant day and even pleasanter evening in countless Maine country towns, squiring about nubile chorines and curious farmers' daughters on constellation-viewing excursions.

They were widely known about the Pine Tree State as sporting men of the old school, enthusiasts of harness racing, wagering and games of chance. And many were the nights when Chick and Lee found themselves in the company of good fellows at any one of the numerous social clubs and organizations for those who had served gallantly in the military.

So, too, they were familiar faces wherever Kiwanians, Rotarians, Odd Fellows, Knights of Pythias, Masons, Moose, Red Men, Eagles and others gathered. It was a rare night for Chick and Lee when they did not seek out that special camaraderie that can be found only where playing cards are shuffled and dice rattled.

On many such outings Chick and Lee would arrive at the evening's destination separately and, fun-loving souls that they were, feign that they were not acquainted. And this made for particularly good sport.

Such outings often led to great fortune at the cards, and it was from such endeavors that both sporting pals returned with an odd variety of winnings, including several cars, a piano, a veritable ark of livestock and an assortment of other booty that included an arsenal of firearms, numerous electrical appliances and a most colorful collection of men's and even women's clothing.

Berlitz had forsaken the world of show business and was now ensconced in the groves of academe as H. Leopold Berlitz, chairman of the Department of Interdisciplinary Studies and an internationally regarded alopecist, the science of curing baldness.

It was the presence of Lee Berlitz among the Abenakians, as well as Chick Devine's winning a deluxe mobile home in a raffle that he had organized, that convinced the road-weary entertainer to winter over in Fillmore.

Now, not very long after the two old troupers had been reunited, Professor Berlitz found himself summoned to meet with Dr. Buford Bassett, longtime president of Abenaki State Teacher's College.

Bassett, then in his early seventies, was famed throughout Maine and as far away as Leominster, Massachusetts, as one of the Pine Tree State's most stalwart educators.

He had guided the school from its days as a two-year teacher's college, then known as Abenaki Normal School, to the present, where it was about to be named the University of Maine at Fillmore.

The college president was also busy with his lifetime effort of creating a scale model of Maine out of popsicle sticks and sugar cubes, and it was hard to this task that the wary Professor Berlitz found him.

Visions of transgressions past danced in the professor's head as he walked into Dr. Bassett's office.

"I understand you have quite a background in the entertainment field?" Bassett said as Lee stood nervously before him, wondering whether he ought to sit down.

"Sit down, sit down," Bassett said.

"That may be a bit of an exaggeration," Lee said.

Bassett was busily spray-painting Piscataquis County a pleasant shade of green. He did not look up.

"I have a little problem on my hands," he said.

"A little problem?"

"A little problem."

"I hope it doesn't involve me," Lee said, easing himself forward in his chair.

"Ah, but it does."

Bassett moved away from his project and walked around his desk, smiling.

"I've been beside myself for weeks, young man. Beside myself. And here you were all along."

He was standing close enough so that Lee could see the hair flaring out of his nostrils and the stains on his tie.

"Don't be evasive with me, Professor Berlitz."

"Evasive?"

"I know all about you. Chick Devine had quite a bit to say."

"Who?"

"Come, come. Don't carry on like this, Professor Berlitz. We have no one to direct this year's college pageant. Did you know that?"

"Pageant? Direct?"

"Well, here you are. Here you are."

"Indeed."

"I suppose you don't know that it carries a nice little stipend too, money left by the poetess Lillian McCrillis Sangerville. She was a daughter of this community. One of the four great poetesses Fillmore has produced."

"Is that a fact?"

"Ora Starbird Varney, Mabel Harte Taylor and Lucille Stiles Boardman were the other three. I wonder if anyone is reading them now?"

"You got me, Dr. Bassett."

"She left a great deal of money, you know. Not from poetry. All her poems were privately published. But her father was Porter Sangerville. I'm sure you've seen that name. Sangerville Mills. Sangerville Paper Company. She was his only heir."

"I see."

"Her will provides for a very generous funding of our annual pageant. Very, very generous."

"What exactly is a pageant?"

"Well, that's part of the problem I was mentioning earlier. You see, Professor Berlitz, Miss Sangerville had some rather, how should I say, old-school ideas about how things should be done. And they are written in, quite carefully written in, to her will, which allocates funding for our annual theatrical event."

Bassett walked slowly around to his desk chair and sat down.

"Miss Sangerville's will stipulates that this funding must be used annually to finance a pageant. I should say an historical pageant, actually."

"An historical pageant?"

"It must be written, conceived, produced and directed here, from scratch. Do you see?"

"And you want me to do this?"

"Chick Devine says there's not a better man for the job."

"Look, Dr. Bassett, I could only do this kind of thing if I had some help, and where could I possibly get help like that up here?"

"Chick Devine has already agreed to help you, so you can see that that's all taken care of."

As it turned out, President Bassett's instructions to Professor Berlitz on the compositions, production and subsequent direction of the grand historical pageant left the former thespian somewhat under the gun to compose a highly original historical drama, replete with songs and interpretive dance, in only ten days.

Facing this monumental task, Lee decided to sequester himself and Chick Devine in the hopes that the muse would descend on them and aid in this artistic endeavor. But before the two bards could hie themselves to a remote hunting camp in the far-off reaches of the Tonsil Lakes, it was necessary to consult with Miss Sangerville's heir and only living relation, her great niece, Miss Charmaine McCrillis Dinsmore, who had been adopted by the old lady as a foundling.

So one afternoon, shortly after the meeting with Dr. Bassett, Lee telephoned Miss McCrillis Dinsmore to arrange for an interview and the imparting of instructions pertinent to the wishes of the late Miss Sangerville's last will and testimony.

As the only living relative of the late poetess, Charmaine McCrillis Dinsmore busied herself administering the massive Sangerville Trust Fund, ably assisted by her great aunt's close friend and longtime legal adviser, Judge Rufus T. Spurgeon.

Miss McCrillis Dinsmore's major concerns involved the annual production of the historical pageant, which she always appeared in; managing the Cape Squab Dinner Theater, where she appeared each summer with her own repertory company, playing all the leading female roles; and restoring her late great-aunt's ancestral home, Forsythia Lodge.

Miss McCrillis Dinsmore was delighted with the news that

professional artistes had been engaged to undertake this year's pageant after so many years of suffering the imbecilities of amateurs. She insisted that Professor Berlitz and Chick Devine take tea with her to discuss their artistic concepts.

"Tea?" asked Chick Devine.

"That's right pal. Tea. Tea for three," said Lee Berlitz.

"Well, it can't hurt."

"This woman is loaded, Chickie. She is rolling in the old moola."

"That's what I like to hear."

"So best behavior, please. No cigars, right?"

"You know me. Scout's honor. Cross my heart."

"And watch what you say. I told her you were an entertainment consultant from out of state. Just play things easy. Right?"

"Don't sweat it. Chick Devine is not a man to drop the ball."

"All you have to do is mention the words *out of state*, and they'll listen."

"I would have thought it was just the opposite. I thought they hated tourists up here."

"Apples and oranges. These folks haven't much use for tourists, but they have no confidence in themselves. They automatically look for an out-of-stater to lead them. And you're just the man for the job."

"Excelsior."

And so it was that Chick Devine and Professor Lee Berlitz came to find themselves sitting in the parlor at Forsythia Lodge, balancing their teacups and chatting most pleasantly with Charmaine McCrillis Dinsmore.

Miss McCrillis Dinsmore, then in her late thirties, was a much younger woman than the Messrs. Berlitz and Devine had expected. Although she had a somewhat severe air about her and was dressed entirely in black, Miss McCrillis Dinsmore was a fine figure of a woman and enchanted with her guests.

"Oh, professor, it's absolutely splendid of you to undertake the pageant. This is just what it has always needed."

"Think nothing of it. I can't wait to get started."

"And where are you from, Mr. Devine?"

"All over, actually. I go where I'm needed—when the arts call."

"Of course."

"I could be in Toledo or Tucson tomorrow. I never know from day to day where the arts will send me."

"It must be a terribly exciting life."

"Oh, it is, but rather lonely at times."

"Yes, but you're serving the arts. Doesn't that make up for the loneliness?"

"Of course, serving the arts. When they call, I go."

"We're just extremely fortunate to have Mr. Devine," said Lee Berlitz.

"Yes, I know, and I'm most grateful," said Miss McCrillis Dinsmore.

"He canceled his entire winter schedule to be with us here."

"Really. Where were you to have been?"

"I'm not at liberty to say, you understand."

"Of course."

"Well, what can we do for you, Miss Dinsmore?" asked Chick Devine.

"Gentlemen, the pageant must meet certain standards. It must be about Maine. Maine history, preferably the history of this region, Abenaki County."

"So we heard," said Lee Berlitz.

"No problem," said Chick Devine.

"Do you have any ideas yet?"

"Plenty of them, but we want to surprise you," said Chick Devine.

"I love surprises."

"You'll love this one," said Chick Devine.

10 ▲ ▲ ▲ ▲ ▲ ▲ ▲ ▲ ▲ ▲

The Boys in the Bateaux, a revisionist view of Maine history, replete with song-and-dance routines and certain performing animals.

Aᴏ̲̈ᴛᴇʀ ᴛʜᴇ ᴘᴀɢᴇᴀɴᴛ was completed, it could never be determined whether it was Chick or Lee who had come up with the idea of composing a musical comedy based on Benedict Arnold's march across Maine to attack the city of Quebec.

Since much of the famous trek took place in Abenaki County, Chick and Lee decided that this was the perfect local angle that could not miss. And with Charmaine McCrillis Dinsmore's blessing they undertook to write such a work.

Certain liberties had to be taken with the actual events, which disturbed the scholar in Lee, but Chick Devine insisted that such bits of poetic license could only improve the production and make history more accessible to the common man.

"There's going to be something in this show for everybody," Chick told Miss McCrillis Dinsmore on the telephone.

"Oh, wonderful. I can't wait."

"The college has never seen the likes of this show. I personally guarantee a sellout every night. Word of honor."

And so the co-authors left for a week-long sojourn at a remote hunting camp in the Tonsil Lakes, borrowed from a card-playing associate, one Armand "Flash" Paradise, a retired woodsman, good sport and former international title holder for the live smelt-eating championship held each year at Tonsil Lakes Lodge.

The camp, Auberge Armand, was located on the backside of the smallest of the Tonsil Lakes, Little Tonsil. Chick and Lee vowed that they would return to civilization in one week's time with the historical opus in working order.

Laboring night and day, the two showmen began hammering out the melodic comedy recounting how Benedict Arnold had bravely led his band of men across the uncharted wilds of Maine and attacked the British in Quebec.

Now, in Chick and Lee's version of this historical milestone Arnold's company was augmented by certain camp followers, which, although not historically accurate, provided some merriment and relieved the boredom the authors felt would definitely occur if they stuck too close to the actual events described by historians.

Accounts of Arnold's trek contained many contradictions and in some cases were based on conjecture and hearsay, as not much was written down at the time. There was, for instance, no proof that Arnold's men were not accompanied by three Indian princesses, and it seemed to Chick and Lee that such traveling companions were certainly within the realm of the possible. And so, Cherry, Jo Anne and Princess Sachem were written in.

So, too, did other inclusions have to be made in reconstructing the march to Quebec. This was, after all, a musical, and who better to assist in that melodic endeavor than Moe Havana's musical charges.

A part was also written for Charmaine McCrillis Dinsmore, and in this account of Arnold's march, the military leader was accompanied by his wife.

As it turned out, all the members of the Fun O'Rama insisted that they be written in. Artists of this kind, being temperamental folk, must be catered to, although many liberties were taken as a result, and purists later criticized the production.

Here is a review by Hennings Condell of the historical pageant as it appeared in the *Portland Post*.

Abenaki State Teacher's College has annually produced a locally written historical pageant in recent years as part of a bequest made to the school by the late poetess Lillian McCrillis Sangerville.

This critic has in previous years found these productions seriously marred by amateurish writing and performing. We have also questioned the point of producing such an archaic and expensive theatrical extravanganza in this day and age.

This year's production, *The Boys in the Bateaux*, is certainly a departure from pageants past. It is, if nothing else, the most unusual theatrical event to be mounted in the state of Maine in our many years of reviewing.

The Boys in the Bateaux purports to be an historically accurate account of the march on Quebec led by Benedict Arnold in which Arnold and his company crossed Maine against great odds and suffered brutal hardships in their campaign against the British. Is there a schoolchild in Maine not familiar with this saga?

In this critic's opinion the musical comedy version of this red-letter date in Maine history bears almost no resemblance to any account of the Arnold march contained in popular accounts.

Extraordinary liberties have been taken with the facts; characters appear in this production who could not possibly have accompanied Arnold and his men.

And that is a good place to start. Men. There is no historical evidence whatsoever, for instance, that Arnold was guided by three Indian princesses. The lead princess, as played by Angela Mannucci, who performs under the stage name of Princess Sachem, the Native American Love Goddess, is most eye-catching.

Her dance numbers brought the house down the night we viewed the pageant, although one of the dances borders dangerously on the risqué and we advise potential pageant-goers that this is not fare for young children. Miss Mannucci's character seemed to become much stimulated by the presence in the audience that night of some two hundred enlisted men from the naval air station at Cape Squab who were said to be there as special guests of the pageant's producer, Mr. Chick Devine.

The princess is joined in her dance numbers by two other performers, "Indian maidens," according to the program notes, played by Cherry St. John and Jo Anne Flambé. Their costumes, consisting of little more than feathers and war paint, and not much of either, bore little resemblance to the traditional garb of Maine's first residents.

In the lead role of Benedict Arnold, college faculty member Professor Lee Berlitz gives a startling if unusual performance that departs radically from the historical events. Berlitz, who speaks with a strong New York accent, addresses the members of Arnold's company as "boys" and laces his dialogue with colloquial expressions not common in the late eighteenth century.

He further departs from the reality by performing a variety of card tricks and other bits of legerdemain at various points during the pageant. On encountering a group of hostile Indians, Berlitz, as Arnold, bribes the savages with cigarette lighters and ballpoint pens.

Also appearing in the production, the producer Chick Devine took the role of Arnold's press agent, a part for which there is most certainly no basis in fact. Devine, the only member of the company not in period costume, halted the production several times to chastise audience members for booing and on one occasion threatened a couple attempting to leave the theater during one of Princess Sachem's saucier gavottes. Devine was loudly cheered at this point by the visiting seamen who were treated to free drinks during the two intermissions.

On another historical note, there is certainly no evidence that Arnold or other members of his expeditionary force wore sunglasses.

Among the most alarming inconsistencies in an alarming and inconsistent production were the inclusion of musicians on the march to Quebec, as well as an Hispanic gentleman and three trained dogs. Surely no one can believe that such members of Arnold's party ever existed.

The musicians, if that is the word, were a quartet of chimpanzees who had been trained to play a small piano, an accordion, the drums and a trumpet. The reader may now be wondering how a piano could possibly have been carried across the forests of Maine during Arnold's expedition.

These musicians, in addition to providing background music, also figured prominently in the march, dressed from head to toe in buckskin.

They did succeed in setting many toes tapping with a spirited rendition of our own Maine Stein Song, but as this was not composed until long after the assault on Quebec, it is improbable that Arnold's men would have sung it. The improbability pales when one considers that during the darkest point of the trek, Arnold's weary band is roused to continue by the musical strains of "Anchors Aweigh." At this point in the production all order in the theater broke down and the seamen in the balcony loudly joined in the singing while several of their obviously intoxicated shipmates appeared on stage. Producer-director Chick Devine appeared to be encouraging all of this.

As written by Chick Devine and Lee Berlitz, this year's pageant is an hallucination from beginning to end, replete with performing dogs, snowmobiles, exotic dancing and, at one point, a display that appeared to be culled from a carnival's freak show.

At one point in the confusing production Charmaine McCrillis Dinsmore, in the role of Mrs. Benedict Arnold, appears on stage and recites a poem by her late great-aunt, Lillian McCrillis Sangerville, which has nothing whatsoever to do with the pageant.

Following this, Chick Devine ran on stage and called out to the audience, "Let's give the little lady a big hand." The sailors in the balcony became most disruptive.

The "grand finale," as it was called, with members of the audience urged to come up on the stage to participate, was almost too much to bear.

(Editor's note: Hennings Condell, substitute teacher, playwright and shoe outlet salesman, is a regular reviewer for the *Post*.)

11 ▲ ▲ ▲ ▲ ▲ ▲ ▲ ▲ ▲

In which we learn of the founding of the Official Maine Guide Correspondence School, a comprehensive mail-order course unlike any other.

IF WARDEN MARLIN "SHADY" VERMOUTH'S WIFE, Viella, hadn't run off with her best friend, Juanita Fredette, and taken every cent the warden had with her—and if Assistant Warden Lucien "Buck" Aroux hadn't already lent Shady every dime he owned, there might never have been an Official Maine Guide Correspondence School. Shady and Buck were pretty desperate, and fortunately for them, Chick Devine was in town to help out.

Truth be told, it was the old Chicker's idea to set the boys up in the mail-order sportsman industry.

A few days after Viella and Juanita got on the southbound bus, Shady and Buck were sitting over at the Chicken Coop, drinking coffee and commiserating on the evils of women.

Viella and Juanita had met the men of their dreams, two sharply dressed arc welders, one evening over at a dance at the Dozing Doe Lounge where they had gone to hear the band Cabin Fever. Shady was up-country at the time and Buck was off, so when the warden got back to the county seat, he found himself to be a bachelor once again, and a poor one too.

Along with lamenting the wiles of women, cheating hearts and arc-welding home wreckers, Shady and Buck were concerned that two recent purchases of theirs, a pair of Polar Panther snowmobiles from Jerry's Liquidation City and Carpet Kingdom, might be repatriated by the seller.

It's one thing in Maine to lose your wife or even your life's savings, but it's quite another thing to have the bank take your snowmobile away.

Now, as it happened on this bleak morning, Chick Devine was sitting down at the other end of the counter taking in this tale of infidelity and financial ruin.

It was then and there that a casual comment from the old showman launched Shady and Buck on a business venture that would make them nationally known.

All over the United States and in many foreign countries there are people today who have never even been to Maine who learned all about the great out-of-doors through the Official Maine Guide Correspondence School, a comprehensive mail-order course unlike any other.

There was some scoffing around Abenaki County when people first heard about the correspondence school. Folks said that no one, not even a veteran warden like Shady Vermouth or a seasoned tracker like Buck Aroux, could teach anyone to be a guide through the mail.

Now, you can go anyplace in the country and you'll see people on the street with their Official Maine Guide Correspondence School windbreakers, or the shoulder patch proudly displayed.

Of course, Shady and Buck, veteran nimrods that they were, had the skills necessary to administer the course, but they would probably still be sitting down at the Chicken Coop waiting for Jerry Velure to take their Polar Panthers away if Chick Devine hadn't come along.

"How the hell can we teach people white-water canoeing through the mail?" asked Shady.

"Or rock climbing or ice fishing?" added Buck.

"Fellas, you're the wardens. I'm just tossing out ideas."

"Look, Chick, we appreciate this, but you can't teach people to be outdoorsmen through the mail. It's a hands-on kind of thing, and it take years, a lifetime," said Shady.

"We was born up here doing this stuff," said Buck.

"That's why you are both eminently qualified to run such a correspondence school."

"I don't know, Chick," said Shady.

"What don't you know?"

"I don't know if this is the answer to our problems. Are people going to want to do this stuff?"

"Are you kidding me, pal? They'll be beating a path to your door," said Chick Devine.

"But this isn't easy to do," said Shady.

"Easy? Of course it's not easy. Nothing in this life is easy, nothing that's really worth it," said Chick Devine. "But you guys can do it. Don't talk to me about easy. You think it's going to be easy for some guy in New York City, the biggest city in the world, to take this course? I mean, here's this guy, all alone in his apartment after a busy day at the office, right? And he's learning how to make a fire in the rain. How easy is that? First off, it's probably illegal in New York City to make a fire in an apartment building. Where's he going to get the proper materials for fire starting? How about simulating rain? That leaves this guy with only one option: he'll have to start the fire in the bathtub with the shower running. How easy is that going to be?"

Chick Devine paused and looked at Shady and Buck.

"This is going to be the toughest mail-order outdoorsman course in the world. White-water canoeing, river rafting, kayaking and lots, lots more. No, it's not going to be easy."

"So how are we going to teach this stuff through the mail?" asked Shady.

"Picture this," said Chick Devine. "Here you are, in your apartment in some high-rise building, learning how to white-water canoe. Maybe you've never even seen a canoe, except in the movies. But there you are, sitting in your apartment, and part nine of the fifteen-part guide's course has just arrived in the mail. And you have to tackle it. Maybe you just finished cleaning up the apartment after last week's installment, starting a fire in the rain. So there you are. Part nine, white-water canoeing. Fortunately for the student, Shady and Buck have sent along some beautiful illustrations, plus lots of maps and step-by-step instructions. And a beautiful orange life vest too. But still, it isn't easy. No siree. You, the novice guide, must take that canoe alone down through those churning, frothing rapids, through those jagged boulders and whirlpools. Tough, huh?"

"Sounds tough to me," said Buck.

"Sounds crazy to me," said Shady.

"But first thing you do is put on that life vest. Now picture this. No canoe, no paddle, no white water. Just the student, alone with the step-by-step, easy-to-follow instructions. That's not tough?" said Chick Devine.

"That's tough," said Buck.

"I don't know about this," said Shady.

"Look, fellas, it's up to you to come up with the specifics. You know the outdoors. You're wardens. Put the program together and let me know how it's going."

"Okay, Chick, we'll get right on it," said Buck.

12 ▲ ▲ ▲ ▲ ▲ ▲ ▲ ▲ ▲

Certain dispatches reveal some difficulties in the operation of the Official Maine Guide Correspondence School.

So SHADY AND BUCK designed the Official Maine Guide Correspondence School and began advertising their services in major metropolitan newspapers around the country. As always, Chick Devine had known a good thing when he saw it, and in no time the boys were swamped with eager would-be outdoorsmen who wanted to hone their guide skills under the tutelage of two of Maine's most experienced woodsmen.

Shady and Buck spent most of their time running the school and devising new courses and course materials for their rapidly expanding number of pupils whose checks and money orders began flowing in.

But they had a few ups and downs as any new business will, and as their adviser Chick Devine was often out of state, they wrote to him to get some counsel.

Dear Chick:

We have had some problems with the mail-order spe-lunking course we told you about in our last letter and have now decided to drop it for the time being.

We may eventually offer it only to advanced-level guides, but for the moment we don't think the students are ready yet. Too many greenhorns have been getting stuck in ventilation shafts and up in the attic. This has resulted in some bad publicity. See attached.

It also may have been a mistake to encourage the guides to practice their woodsy skills in public places, especially in Central Park down in New York City. Also see attached.

Some of those guides have been dressing up in a bear suit and putting a group of tenderfoots through their paces. They have also been having hunts and tracking sessions on weekends, and these are getting out of hand. There have been some arrests, you know. See attached.

We have repeatedly warned the guides that it is wrong and a violation of the Official Maine Guide Correspondence School oath for them to involve innocent civilians and domestic animals in their field maneuvers unbeknownst to those parties, but you know how some spoil it for all.

The Cleveland chapter of the guides got a bad write-up in the newspaper out there after they stalked a Lhasa apso with dye guns one Saturday morning. But that incident was exaggerated, and that little dog wasn't hurt one bit, just badly scared. As you can see from this month's guides' newsletter, *Notes 'Round the Camp Fire*, we are thinking about revoking the Cleveland group's charter if they don't behave themselves.

We are still working on the official handshake and moose call, and your buddy, Lee Berlitz, over at the college, is writing an Official Maine Guide Correspondence School song. So, as you can see, there are some good things happening in addition to our difficulties. Hope to get the bugs worked out of this very soon. Please write and let us know when you'll be back in Abenaki County.

Your pals,
Shady and Buck

Dear Shady and Buck:

It's easy to laugh at those eager-beaver correspondence school students who got a little carried away and tried to use their white-water skills right away before certification by the school's board of veteran guides.

I've seen those pictures from the newspapers you sent me of people sitting in rented canoes in public fountains and duck ponds. Let people laugh all they want. Those guides mean well. I say give them all A for effort.

I know all about the rock-climbing and ice-climbing problems and the spelunking. I think you made the right move dropping that installment, might have been a tad advanced for the pupils. Some of these things are bound to happen, despite your best efforts. After all, it says right on the manual, "Do not attempt to duplicate rock-climbing conditions in your apartment building."

Can't they read?

I know there have been a few mishaps, but not to worry. The one bad accident from the rock-climbing course can hardly be blamed on you boys.

That guy was not even an officially enrolled student. He heard about the course on TV and tried to pirate the course materials. Well, he's going to be okay, but let's hope that others learn from his misfortune.

And let's take a moment right now, while I think of it, to make sure you thank those firemen for getting that guy down off the side of that building.

You've got to stress with all of the guides that they must not attempt to master rock-climbing in their apartment buildings without proper training. The life you save . . . right?

Keep an eye on that outfit in Cleveland. I don't like the sound of things out there.

Well, so long for now, I can't wait to hear the official song. Be home soon.

Your pal,
Chick Devine

13 ▲ ▲ ▲ ▲ ▲ ▲ ▲ ▲ ▲

The professor takes a bride. And several reports of the nuptials appear in the popular press.

B<small>Y THE TIME</small> Chick Devine got back to Maine, he found an even bigger surprise awaiting him than the doings over at the Official Maine Guide Correspondence School.

While the impresario had been in the nation's southland attending to matters of fun for the whole family, his old pal and confidant, Lee Berlitz, had up and planned to wed. Unbeknownst to most of the residents of Abenaki County, the good professor had been keeping company with the fair Charmaine McCrillis Dinsmore for some months.

"Wedding bells are about to be ringing. This is grand news, indeed," said Chick Devine.

"We're planning on doing this up big, Chick. Real big," said Lee Berlitz.

"I would expect nothing less from a man of your breeding, sir."

"Of course, your services will be needed. You know that."

"I'll clear the decks for this blessed occasion."

The wedding was the biggest bash that the county seat had seen in many moons, and the following is an account of the grand event as reported by Mrs. Inez Huff, local correspondent for the *Portland Post* and society editor for the *Abenaki Clarion*, which ran a special edition to coincide with the uniting of the fairest flower of Fillmore with the learned H. Leopold Berlitz, professor of interdisciplinary studies.

CHARMAINE McCRILLIS DINSMORE WEDS PROFESSOR H. LEOPOLD BERLITZ

by Inez Huff
Regional Correspondent

Miss Charmaine McCrillis Dinsmore was wed here Saturday to Professor H. Leopold Berlitz in a double-ring ceremony at the Rock of Ages Hall and drew well-wishers from near and far.

Mr. Chick Devine, operator of Chick Devine's Fun O'Rama, served as best man, while Lorraine Fontaine, owner of Fontaine's School of Cosmetology, was maid of honor.

She was ably assisted in that capacity by three of the most darling girls to have ever graced the wedding chapel at the Rock of Ages Hall, the Misses Cherry St. John, Jo Anne Flambé and Princess Sachem.

The bride was given in marriage by retired Judge Rufus T. Spurgeon, longtime friend of the family.

Lucien "Buck" Aroux, assistant game warden and dean of students at the Official Maine Guide Correspondence School, served as ring bearer, and a guard of honor was arranged by Warden Marlin "Shady" Vermouth, chancellor of the Official Maine Guide Correspondence School.

That company included Vernon "Buster" Flagg; Vaughn "Junior" Flagg; Victor, Wayne and Duane Fontaine; and Pepe Baraja.

The Reverend Dr. Don Olay joined the couple in holy matrimony, and a bountiful nuptial fete followed at the

Odd Fellows Hall, splendidly catered by the Jolly Christians ladies' auxiliary, headed by Francelia Spurgeon.

Many out-of-state guests were in attendance, including Ferlin Mosher, a distant relation of the bride, who visited from Fitchburg, Massachusetts.

State Representative Jerome B. "Jerry" Velure (R–Abenaki), was also on hand to present the lovely couple with a special gubernatorial proclamation in honor of the auspicious occasion.

Music was provided by Rene LaRocke's Accordion Rascals, courtesy of the Crystal Lounge. A special musical entertainment was also provided by the Messrs. Morris, Melvin and Morton Havana of Ocalala, Florida, and Fillmore, Maine, who brought a quartet of musically inclined monkeys who cheered the partygoers with a rousing version of our own Maine Stein Song, as well as playing a number of requests.

These amusing little animals were especially enjoyed by the younger members of the wedding party, and they made a very nice appearance dressed as they were in little dinner jackets. They also displayed most excellent table manners and further delighted revelers by smoking cigars during the band break.

Many toasts were made, and a special benediction was offered in French by Father Romeo Bissonette, pastor of the Church of the Goodsportsman.

After a honeymoon trip to Lac Megantic, P.Q., the newlyweds plan to reside at least part of the year here in Fillmore and the remainder at the Cape Squab Dinner Theater.

The affair was one of the most elaborate wedding parties ever seen here in the county seat, and a wonderful time was had by all.

Mrs. Huff's article appeared on the front page of the *Abenaki Clarion* along with three photographs of the wedding party.

One photo showed Professor Berlitz and Charmaine coming down the front steps of the Rock of Ages Hall while the honor guard held an arc of snowshoes for them to walk through.

The second showed the lovely couple hosting a receiving line and greeting visitors, including Grand-Uncle Mosher and Pepe Baraja, who had brought along Lu Lu, Chi Chi and Pepita.

The final photograph showed the celebrants dancing the night away while Moe Havana's little charges made music.

A briefer version of the wedding account appeared in the Portland newspaper, which used only a much out-of-focus head shot of the bride.

However, news of the nuptials did reach many out-of-state points after a Boston newspaper ran a brief story under the headline MONKEYS MAKE MUSIC AS MAINERS MARRY. The photograph showing Moe Havana's quartet entertaining was widely distributed and prompted many inquiries, including a letter from officials at the National Geographic Society.

14

Certain biographical material pertaining to the Fontaine brothers and how they came to lose five state troopers from New Jersey.

Between augusta and the Canadian line, the Fontaine brothers were perhaps Maine's best-known siblings. Their misdeeds were the stuff of legends, and no police officer, deputy sheriff, state trooper, game warden, town constable or fire marshal between Cornville and Coburn Gore had not at some time encountered Victor, Wayne and Duane Fontaine in the line of duty.

In the card catalog at the District Court in Fillmore, the Fontaines' transgressions ran the gamut from animal cruelty to urinating in public, with stops in between at night-hunting, breaking and entering, assault with intent to kill, and possession of stolen property. There was a separate file for motor vehicle violations.

Victor was the oldest and most feared, although both he and brother Wayne were alumni of the Men's Correctional Training Center and had gone on to do graduate work at the Maine State Prison at Thomaston.

But two years of making bird feeders had failed to dull the

brothers' tastes for mischief or instill in them an interest in ornithology.

While brothers Victor and Wayne were guests of the state, the youngest member of the trio, Duane, completed his studies at Abenaki State Teacher's College and began teaching general science at the regional high school. The position had actually been advertised as that of a wrestling coach.

The Fontaines lived near town on a hillside in what had once been a fine old farm. But thirty years of studied neglect had left Fontaine Hill Farm looking shabby and abandoned although the boys still called it home.

The front lawn and side yards were littered with the remains of innumerable cars, pickup trucks and pieces of farm machinery, along with dozens of appliances.

Various fires had taken their toll of the outbuildings, and the roof on the great barn, which still bore the date 1790, sagged wearily.

All of the fields of what had once been a six-hundred-acre showplace had been allowed to grow over, along with a once profitable apple orchard. The first Fontaine had come up to the valley to claim this land following meritorious service in the Revolutionary War, and the family had prospered and served with distinction hereabouts. The walls of the courthouse and town hall were lined with the yellowed photographs of Fontaine clan members past, pillars of the community.

Victor, Wayne and Duane were doing their best to reverse the historic trend, following studiously in the footsteps of their dear old father, Bert Fontaine, a legendary night-hunter and scofflaw who left town under unusual circumstances while the boys were still very young. Their grandmother raised them and their older sister, Lorraine, the cosmetologist and educator.

Since the age of sixteen, the legal age at which one needs to worry no further about pursuing one's studies in the public schools of Maine, Victor and Wayne had busied themselves tinkering with cars, some of which actually belonged to them, and operating a body shop in a cinder-block garage, constructed during a burst of ambition at Fontaine Hill Farm.

Their free time was spent at Tri-County Raceway where both Victor and Wayne had won something of a reputation for their skills as stock-car drivers with no regard for human life, their own or others.

In addition to being the oldest, Victor, then in his mid-thirties, was also the smallest of the trio. He was a wiry five foot six, his hair cut down close to his scalp, a hairstyle once much favored for hygienic reasons at correctional facilities. For some reason or other, even on rare occasions when he had spruced himself up for a court date or a visit with his parole officer, Victor always looked like he needed a shave. Numerous pugilistic encounters in bottle clubs and roadhouses had taken some of the punch out of Victor's smile. His front teeth were missing.

Brother Wayne was a size larger but cut along the same lines, although he wore his hair in a long ponytail.

Among the distinguishing marks on Victor and Wayne were a series of hand-done tattoos, artwork resulting from their extended stays behind bars. On the three largest knuckles of Victor's hands the letters VIC had been inked.

Brother Duane was a neater version of the other two, who never went anywhere without a toothpick in his mouth.

The brothers also devoted themselves to the great outdoors and in that pursuit had become the focus of considerable attention from the state warden service over the years.

In the fall, whenever possible, the Fontaines took parties of unsuspecting sports, out-of-state nimrods and big-game enthusiasts out into the woods.

It was in this capacity, as the operators of Fontaine's

Hunting Lodge, that they had the great misfortune to lose five state troopers from New Jersey.

The exact circumstances were never clear. However, based on previous outings the brothers had conducted, we can say with reasonable assurance that alcoholic beverages and a lack of supervision played a role.

The brothers weren't actually at the campsite up on the west branch of the Slate River at the time the five troopers vanished. Wayne had made an emergency run to the county seat for ice, and brothers Victor and Duane were busily engaged in putting out salt licks and apples in hopes of drawing some big game, practices discouraged by the fish and game authorities.

Fact is, the five troopers had been missing a whole day before the shamefaced Fontaine brothers drove back down to the county seat and told Shady and Buck that they had lost their hunting party.

The brothers had tried in vain to track the missing troopers by following a trail of empty beer cans through the woods, but the trail got cold when the troopers ran out of beer.

15 ▲ ▲ ▲ ▲ ▲ ▲ ▲ ▲ ▲

The great search for the missing hunting party is aided by the unexpected arrival of certain out-of-state visitors.

N o ONE CAN SAY that the state of Maine left any stones un-turned in its attempt to find those roaming lawmen from the Garden State.

Warden Marlin "Shady" Vermouth and his trusted assistant, Lucien "Buck" Aroux, did their utmost.

It may be easy now, in retrospect, to criticize, as it was for most of the daily newspapers in New Jersey at the time of the search. Hindsight is a wonderful thing.

Shady and Buck said later that they may have erred when they put out the call for all available graduates of the Official Maine Guide Correspondence School to come to the aid of the search effort.

Of course, no one thought much would come of that until three chartered busloads of guides rolled into the search site. Most of the guides had never been up to Maine before, some had never been more than a few blocks from home, and none of them had actually ever been in the woods. Fortunately they all had the good sense to bring along all of the manuals and instruction kits that Shady and Buck had sold them.

Every single one of them, man and boy, was decked out in their Official Maine Guide Correspondence School uniform. If nothing else, that was a mighty impressive thing to see.

"What in the hell is this?" asked Shady.

"You got me," said Buck.

Both wardens were weary after another long day of searching without success. Shady, Buck, and the Fontaine brothers were sitting on the porch of Fontaine's Hunting Lodge having a smoke and discussing where the missing hunters could have gone.

The remainder of the search effort, including state police Corporal Birchell Huff, husband of Inez Huff, Buster and Junior Flagg and the poet Vance Lancet, were still in the woods.

The search was beginning to capture the imagination of the community, in no small part because of the lively dispatches of Mrs. Inez Huff, who was assisted in their composition by Chick Devine, who had appointed himself special press liaison.

Jerry Velure had sent Cliff Leach with a wagonload of equipment so that listeners to WEZY AM-FM, the voice of Abenaki County, could be informed up to the minute on the hour and half hour about the comings and goings at the search site, brought to them as a public service by Jerry's Liquidation City and Carpet Kingdom.

Chick Devine had also enlisted the services of Cherry St. John, Jo Anne Flambé and Princess Sachem, not to mention Pepe Baraja and the pups, Lu Lu, Chi Chi and Pepita.

Francelia Spurgeon and Lorraine Fontaine headed up a delegation from the Jolly Christians in the dispensing of assorted baked goods and dry socks to members of the rescue effort.

And so it was when the three busloads of Official Maine Guide Correspondence School graduates arrived.

Buck walked down to where the buses were parked, to quiz

the new arrivals, and was back in record time.

"Shady, you know what we got here, pal?"

"Who are those guys?"

"Those are our boys, Shady. Official Maine Guide Correspondence School graduates, in uniform."

"I can't believe this. There must be two hundred of them. What are we going to do?" said Shady.

"One hundred and eighty-seven, all present and accounted for," said Buck.

The leader of the guides and their spokesman was one Louis Apponzio, a frequent correspondent with Buck and Shady who signed his dispatches "Ranger Lou."

But neither Buck nor Shady had ever laid eyes on Ranger Lou or, for that matter, on any of their hundreds of devoted correspondents.

Ranger Lou, in his official uniform, was a short, solid little man, sweating heavily under the weight of the massive load of field equipment he had brought along. He was also wearing his orange life vest, the one supplied for white-water canoeing lessons.

"Well, well, Ranger Lou, at long last, after all this time. I'm Assistant Warden Aroux. Just call me Buck."

"Right you are, Buck," said Ranger Lou.

"And this is Warden Vermouth, the chancellor of the Official Maine Guide Correspondence School. And these gentlemen are Wayne, Duane and Victor Fontaine. I suppose you could call them visiting scholars at the school."

"Men, it's good to be here," said Ranger Lou.

Shady could not speak but continued to stare, first at Ranger Lou and then at the dozens and dozens of Ranger Lou look-alikes in various shapes and sizes, all weighted down under vast quantities of Official Maine Guide Correspondence School camping equipment, an arsenal of firearms, entrenching tools, tent poles, fishing equipment and portable toilets.

Buck Aroux was already a step ahead of his bewildered colleague.

"Ranger Lou, return to your squads and have your men stand at ease until we can give them their assignments," Buck said.

"Sir," said Ranger Lou, and off he went.

"He follows orders," Buck said to Shady.

"Thank God for that."

"What if headquarters in Augusta finds out these guys are up here helping out? What if they find out about the school?" said Buck.

"I don't know what we're going to do with them," said Shady.

Because Shady and Buck feared that the guides might be more of a danger to themselves and others as well as a severe hindrance to the search effort, they decided to tie groups of them together with a heavy-test orange twine they were using to mark off search areas. They reasoned that it would be much harder to lose a group of guides and therefore easier to account for their visitors.

"They won't be able to move too fast all tied up like that. Less chance that they'll wander off, especially carrying all that equipment," said Buck.

So Shady and Buck, with some help from the Fontaine brothers, lined up all of the guides, with the exception of several very elderly ones, and strung them together in groups of twenty or so with the twine looped around the right wrist of each guide. And when the search resumed, Shady and Buck took a stringload each, and Buster and Junior Flagg were also pressed into service and warned not to lose a single guide.

Chick Devine remained at the command post with a band of guides deemed too frail for a day of traipsing through the woods.

16

The Official Maine Guide Correspondence School attracts un-warranted attention.

ABOUT HALFWAY THROUGH the second week of the search, Warden Inspector Merton Spicer arrived at the search site on an errand from the governor's office. It seemed that the governor of New Jersey had been in contact about the missing troopers. And Governor Harland Payson Getchell wanted some idea of how the manhunt was progressing.

As luck would have it, Warden Inspector Spicer just showed up unannounced, and his report reflects this.

> I arrived at the search site on the west branch of the Slate River on property belonging to the Colburn Paper Company at approximately 0800 hours, October 11.
>
> On first entering the search site, I was made to stop my vehicle and present identification by two individuals, whom I later learned were Vernon "Buster" Flagg and Vaughn "Junior" Flagg, operators of the rural mail service in Abenaki County.
>
> At the center of the campsite Warden Marlin Vermouth and Assistant Warden Lucien Aroux were engaged in lin-

ing up dozens of men dressed in paramilitary uniforms and heavily laden with assorted pieces of camping equipment.

Unaware of my presence, the warden and his assistant then proceeded to tie up these men into groups of twenty, linking them together with orange twine.

While this was going on, two women passed out box lunches to the men, whom I later learned were graduates of an organization unknown to me, the Official Maine Guide Correspondence School.

Three other subjects, whom I later learned were Wayne, Duane and Victor Fontaine, were some distance from the main party, sitting in a parked car where I observed them drinking alcoholic beverages, expressly forbidden during such procedures. The Fontaine brothers are known to this department as habitual offenders of state fish-and-game law.

An older man wearing a business suit, who later identified himself as Chick Devine and presented me with one of his business cards, which read, "The Chick Devine Fun O'Rama," was passing along the line of guides, shaking each man's hand. He was accompanied by three young women in full-length fur coats, who proceeded to kiss and otherwise embrace the members of the search party.

A short distance from the main group, an elderly gentleman was speaking in a language which I believe was Spanish to three small dogs that were wearing orange life vests.

The campsite was in great disarray at the time of my arrival, with the majority of the members of the guides breaking into song periodically. They were directed by a guide who was the apparent leader of this group, one Ranger Lou, also known as Louis Apponzio, an assistant produce manager at a supermarket in Levittown, Long Island.

Due to the general confusion and substantial disarray in the campsite, I was able to wander about without my presence becoming immediately known to Warden Vermouth or Assistant Warden Aroux.

Apparently the Official Maine Guide Correspondence School is operated from a post office box in Abenaki County by Warden Vermouth and Assistant Warden Aroux. According to literature that I obtained at the search site, Vermouth and Aroux have been teaching so-called "Maine woods lore" through the mail for some period, primarily to enthusiasts in urban areas.

I was also able to obtain a large selection of the literature distributed by the school, purporting to instruct subscribers "in the ways of the deep woods." I have enclosed several examples, including selections on white-water canoeing, tracking in the dark, and animal and bird calls.

The guides present at the campsite on the morning of my visit explained that they had been asked to come to Maine by Warden Vermouth when he put out some sort of nationwide call. A company of nearly two hundred of them, many heavily armed, were at the campsite on the morning of my visit.

According to Ranger Lou, whom I interviewed at length as he was not participating in the active search but helping a group of elderly women known as the Jolly Christians to make sandwiches, the group of guides present, was, in his words, "just the tip of the iceberg."

Ranger Lou alleged that Warden Vermouth and Assistant Warden Aroux, as heads of the Official Maine Guide Correspondence School, have a nationwide following of these enthusiasts, possibly numbering in the thousands.

Warden Inspector Spicer did not bother to interview Buck and Shady, having already jumped to unfortunate conclusions about what was going on out at the search site. Driving hard, he was back in Augusta late that same day, where he made his report to Chief Warden Munroe Falconer.

The next morning, by the time they got over to the governor's office, things were really starting to get out of hand.

A news conference was called, a few photographs that Warden Inspector Spicer had taken were distributed and one thing led to another.

The Portland paper used the story on its front page the next morning, along with a photograph of the guides being strung together. It ran under the headline STATE CONCERNED ABOUT PARAMILITARY GROUP LED BY MAINE WARDENS.

Governor Harland Payson Getchell yesterday called on the head of the Maine Warden Service to explain why an alleged paramilitary group was being used to conduct a search for five missing hunters from New Jersey.

The missing hunters, all New Jersey state troopers, disappeared without a trace two weeks ago while at a hunting camp in the remote west branch section of the Slate River. The land, owned by the Colburn Paper Company, is among Maine's most impenetrable woods, and no sign of the missing troopers has been uncovered.

According to a spokesman for the governor's office, an independent check on the status of the search was done yesterday.

Warden Inspector Merton Spicer, who briefed reporters, said he found the search site "in a great state of confusion."

Spicer told a statehouse news conference late yesterday that some two hundred heavily armed men, calling themselves members of the Official Maine Guide Correspondence School, were camped out at the search site. The men alleged that they were under the direction of Warden Marlin Vermouth and Assistant Warden Lucien Aroux. State officials were unable to contact either man for additional comment, but Spicer said the guides told him that they had been "recruited from out of state."

In addition, Spicer told reporters that "numerous irregularities were found at the search site." He charged that searchers were openly consuming alcoholic beverages and that the area had sustained "major environmental damage."

Spicer also reported that a number of civilians were at the search site, including the operator of a carnival, three young women, several members of a church service organization, two rural mail carriers and an Hispanic man with three trained dogs.

"I've never seen anything like it in all my years in the service," the veteran warden said.

"You've got a dangerous situation up there. You've got two hundred heavily armed men, and I just don't know what they're capable of doing."

Chief Warden Munroe Falconer vowed to fully investigate the entire situation.

Meanwhile, a spokesman for Governor Getchell said the state would be contacting the provincial government in neighboring Quebec to apprise officials there of the situation. The search site where the paramilitary group is camped is only five miles from the Canadian border.

"We just want our neighbors to the north to know that we are aware of this situation and want to allay any fears that they may have about a possible armed invasion from this state," the spokesman said.

The television station down in Portland took a slightly different approach to the story. Their statehouse correspondent, Rick Bass, who headed up the station's special investigative team, "The Eye Strike Force," made a few phone calls and then told Maine viewers that "an estimated five hundred armed commandos are camped in the deep woods."

The eager Bass, who also worked as a stringer for other news organizations, then filed a dispatch with a Boston newspaper, which in turn passed the information on to the wire services.

Two days after the news conference this dispatch was appearing in daily newspapers from sea to shining sea.

COMMANDOS' LAIR FOUND
IN MAINE'S DEEP WOODS

A group of more than one thousand heavily armed commandos, believed to be Vietnam-era veterans unable to adjust to life in the United States, has been found at a remote site in the deep woods of Maine near the Canadian border.

Authorities in Maine believe the men are professional killers and survivalists who are living off the land owned by a large paper company.

"These guys are mad-dog killers. They are wild animals. At this point in time we are just studying the situation to determine how to positively facilitate our response," a police spokesman who asked not to be identified told reporters.

Officials believe the paramilitary group may be planning to move drugs or nuclear weapons across the border from nearby Quebec. The group may also be linked to a separatist attempt to seize a portion of rural Maine and set up an independent country.

17 ▲ ▲ ▲ ▲ ▲ ▲ ▲ ▲ ▲ ▲

How a public relations dilemma was solved by a stitch in time.

THE FIRST WORD Shady and Buck had of the "public relations problem," as Chick Devine termed it, was when the roving Chicker turned up again at the search site with some copies of the press the boys were getting downstate.

"Mad-dog killers?" said Shady.

"Survivalists?" said Buck.

"What the hell is going on here?" asked Shady.

"Fellas, near as I can figure, what you've got here is what we used to call a 'public relations problem' or, better, 'crisis' back at the old Fun O'Rama," said Chick Devine.

"What're we going to do now?" asked Shady.

"Calm yourselves. The way I see it is to get rid of the guides. They're drawing all the flies. Hell, if you didn't have them up here, you would've never hit the papers," said Chick.

"It's not that easy, Chick," said Buck.

"They won't leave," said Shady.

"We've asked them to leave," added Buck.

"They've sworn the Official Maine Guide Correspondence School oath that they will not rest or retire from the field until the missing troopers are found," said Shady.

"So what's the problem? Find the troopers and declare the search over," said Chick.

"That's not so easy," said Shady.

"Boys, as a specialist in the field of public relations crises, I must advise you that there is only one way to fight a public relations crisis. Head-on. With another public relations crisis," said Chick Devine.

"What do you propose?" asked Buck.

"What we need here is a little showmanship," said Chick Devine.

And so it was the Pepe Baraja and the Havana brothers were outfitted with shears and needle and thread. A search of the missing lawmen's Winnebago had uncovered five New Jersey state police uniforms.

"Time for some alterations, gentlemen," said Chick Devine.

To look now at the photograph that Inez Huff took of Roger Caron and the four chimps dressed as state troopers, you can hardly tell the difference. Chick Devine knew what he was doing.

First off, he stood the chimps up on top of a picnic table and then had several of their "rescuers"—Buck, Shady and the Fontaine brothers—stand or sit in front of them.

"This'll make the chimps look taller," said Chick Devine.

As Inez Huff was not quite the photographer she could have been, she produced a very passable likeness, which viewed at just the right distance showed five heavily bearded state troopers back in civilization after a harrowing two weeks of being lost in Maine's deep woods. Roger Caron, in the supporting role of the fifth state trooper, lacked the chimp's enthusiasm for this theatrical effort, but a good talking-to by Chick Devine raised his spirits.

While all of this was being done, Ranger Lou and the men and boys of the Official Maine Guide Correspondence School expeditionary force were off in the woods in the custody of other members of the search party. *Heartbroken* is not too strong a word to use to describe the way Ranger Lou and his band felt when they returned to camp to find that not only had the missing lawmen been found safe and sound, but also that they had left already.

And so it was that the guides, weighted down with memorabilia from their trek into the Pine Tree State, prepared to return to civilization.

Battle mementos and other souvenirs of the good fight were all around. Ranger Lou, himself, was typical of the members of the outfit, for in addition to the great mass of camping equipment with which he had outfitted himself for trending into Maine, there were now many items representative of Maine life.

Each guide had strapped a lobster trap to the top of his pack, which made walking a task. There were also lobster buoys, loads of driftwood and a goodly number of sporting trophies—racks of antlers and the mounted heads of moose and deer. An entire stuffed black bear was lashed to the roof of one of the buses.

Chick Devine and Jerry Velure, with the assistance of a prominent taxidermist with a cash-flow problem, had been able to obtain a variety of deep-woods trophies for the guides and pass them on to them at a "substantial savings," as the old Chicker put it.

Near the departure area, Inez Huff had set up a table to take down addresses for the official portrait of the expedition.

Chick Devine, whom many of the guides had taken to calling Commander Devine, reviewed the troops and offered a brief, inspirational address, copies of which would also be made available at a later date for a small fee.

18 ▲ ▲ ▲ ▲ ▲ ▲ ▲ ▲ ▲

The Saga of the Wily Coyoon, a vicious predator of the Maine woods.

THE FIRST THING Warden Marlin "Shady" Vermouth and his trusted associate and Assistant Warden Lucien "Buck" Aroux did in the morning when they stopped in at the Chicken Coop for breakfast was to open up the sports pages to read the outdoors column, "Maine Stream," by the sage of the wilderness, Gorham "Bub" Varney.

Bub Varney was not only a veteran outdoorsman and writer whose reports on field and stream were nationally syndicated, but also he was the host of *Bub's Rucksack,* an hour-long television program sponsored by Jerry's Liquidation City and Carpet Kingdom.

Surveys taken by Maine's television stations had repeatedly shown that Bub Varney's program, now in its twentieth year, was among the top three most popular shows in the state.

Bub Varney was the man to talk to when it came to the out-of-doors. From Eastport to Eagle Lake, whenever there was sporting news being made, Bub Varney was on the scene. Bub and his wife, Darlene, virtually lived in their camper as they crossed the back roads and byways of Maine, keeping tabs on flora and fauna.

Old Uncle Bub was a fixture among public speakers as well and there was hardly a Kiwanis prayer breakfast, a baked bean supper or a fireman's field day in any part of Maine where Bub Varney had not regaled young and old alike with his tales of back-country adventures.

His television program, with its open phones, served as the unofficial sounding board for any and all matters pertaining to wildlife, hunting, fishing, trapping and traipsing.

Any candidate for statewide office was assured of an easier time with the blessing of Bub Varney and an appearance on *Bub's Rucksack* was an imprimatur avidly sought by anyone with political aspirations.

With his ever-present coffee cup from which he sipped with increasing regularity as the evening wore on, the ruddy-faced Uncle Bub, always in his rumpled flannel shirt and fishing vest, pronounced on all matters and on friend and foe alike.

Bub's Rucksack did not confine itself to matters of field and stream but also roved off into other terrain. Bub Varney was not afraid to tackle the evils around him.

Among the regular guests on the *Rucksack*, in addition to veteran wardens and guides, were some of Maine's best-known sporting personalities and, frequently, surprise guests.

Just about every year, come hunting season, Bub Varney could produce a Maine resident with an unusual tale to tell about hunting. And no one was more popular among Uncle Bub's regular gang of guests than ninety-year-old Farlin Dow, who, though confined to a wheelchair and now legally blind, was still regarded as one of the three or four best shots in the State o' Maine.

Only last year, at eighty-nine years young, Farlin Dow had

shot an eleven-hundred-pound bull moose from his wheelchair and then dressed the critter out without a bit of help. National television programs had been up to cover the event.

By God, when Bub Varney and Farlin Dow and some of the other old woodsmen got to jawing on *Rucksack*, listeners got to really hear some tales of the Maine woods when Maine was still Maine, as Uncle Bub would say, before all these damn out-of-staters started coming up here with all their notions.

Out-of-staters, even out-of-state hunters, were in for some rough sledding when Uncle Bub Varney and Farlin Dow took to sipping on their coffee and opinionating.

During the hunting season Uncle Bub always liked to have some game wardens on the show to tell the most unusual story that they had about out-of-state hunters, and many of these tales were Bub Varney classics, which longtime viewers liked to hear retold. Some of the yarns had been collected into a hilarious, but true-life, anthology of amusing hunting accidents called *Shoot First, Ask Questions Later*, a perfect gift for the hunter in your life.

Just as Farlin Dow's visits were occasions of sporting merriment, Bub Varney loved to have Chief Warden Munroe Falconer on each October to tell about the time he was working at a tagging station up near Hainesville when a carload of hunters from Connecticut rolled in to report that one of their band had bagged a "midget deer." Munroe always built up to the climax by explaining in great detail and quite slowly how he sauntered on outside to the Nimrods' vehicle, and at this point in the story he would always hold up a black-and-white eight-by-ten photograph he had kept and cherished ever since.

The photo, taken by another warden, showed the four visiting hunters standing around a good-sized goat. Munroe posed the nimrods for the picture before he explained to them that this was no midget deer they had.

Further fun ensued at the tagging station when the elderly

lady who owned the goat arrived fit to be tied and reported that her pet had been bagged while eating his way along the roadside not a hundred yards from her front door.

Every year, come hunting season, Bub Varney would have a camera crew out filming farmers all over Maine as they spray-painted their livestock orange and placed large fluorescent signs in English and French reading, DON'T KILL ME, I AM A COW.

There were plenty of good times to be had watching *Bub's Rucksack*, and nothing was more fun than when Bub butted heads with some of his more critical callers. A few rounds with Uncle Bub would take the wind out of even the most avid environmentalist's sails.

Uncle Bub could get a bit nasty if he'd had more coffee than usual, and a couple of times the station manager had had to come on at the end of the *Rucksack* to advise listeners that Uncle Bub's opinions were not necessarily those of the management of the station.

But there was never a better-loved man in the great State of Maine than Uncle Bub Varney, a real tough guy with a heart of gold. Every summer he hosted Uncle Bub's Buddies, groups of underprivileged kids from the inner city who came up to Maine for a few weeks of fresh air.

All of the newspapers would always run a picture of Uncle Bub welcoming his little pals from Boston and New York.

He was a man of many contrasts, the buddy of many under-privileged kids, the sage of the outdoors to many, many sports-men, while others thought more strongly about Uncle Bub.

"Troglodyte," said the poet Vance Lancet one morning, sitting in the Chicken Coop, chatting with Buck and Shady.

"I don't think that's any of our business," said Shady.

"Behind closed doors it's up to him," said Buck.

The conversation between Buck and Shady and the poet Vance Lancet was prompted by a column Buck was trying to read aloud to those assembled for breakfast that morning.

The announcement that Bub Varney's column was about to be read aloud had prompted scorn from Vance, who rarely said a discouraging word about anyone.

"Listen to this, Shady," said Buck.

"I'm all ears, pal," said the warden.

STRANGE CREATURE REPORTED IN NORTHWESTERN MAINE

Veteran guide and tracker Victor "Vic" Fontaine knows Maine's woods like few other outdoorsmen. So he is not easily surprised by anything he might encounter while on the trail. But this was not the case a few days ago up on the Colburn Paper Company private road near Bald Pate Notch.

Vic told this column that he and his close friend, Armand "Flash" Paradise, who some may know for his exploits as the longtime international title holder in the live smelt-swallowing championship held each year at the Tonsil Lake Lodge, had encountered a varmint long believed extinct in the Maine woods.

While driving along the paper company road near dusk Vic and Flash spied an animal about the size of a German shepherd in the distance. On closer examination the animal appeared to have the facial characteristics of a raccoon. Startled by the vehicle, the critter stood up on its back legs and hissed at Vic and Flash before running off on all fours into the woods.

Old-timers and faithful readers of this column will know that what Vic and Flash had happen to them up near Bald Pate Notch was a rare sighting of a creature that once roamed the Maine woods in great numbers, the coyoon, a cross between a coyote and a raccoon, known in the western states as a raccote.

Fish and game experts along the eastern seaboard have long believed this creature extinct east of the Mississippi.

The last official sighting of the coyoon in Maine was back in 1963, when the outdoorsman Farlin Dow, one of Maine's legendary nimrods, spotted a pair of coyoons near the town dump in Mercer.

The coyoon is as crafty a critter as any that this columnist has encountered in the Maine woods, because it has traits and habits common to both the coyote and the raccoon. Just as coyotes are well-known to chase deer and even domestic livestock, and raccoons are famed for their ability as scroungers in the garbage, the coyoon is worse than either. Coyoons will chase garbage trucks.

The popularity of inexpensive metal garbage cans was thought to be responsible for the critter's demise in the East. But coyoonologists now believe that the trend toward plastic trash bags, which afford coyoons easy access, has led to their return in growing numbers.

Not three days after Vic and Flash spotted that lone coyoon on the road up near Bald Pate Notch, this columnist received a late-night phone call from Ora Hatch, fire warden at Mount Seboomadnoc. Another coyoon had been sighted.

This columnist believes that the recent banning of disposable plastic trash bags in Canada has driven these creatures down into Maine in search of food. We hope to act as a clearinghouse for any further information that readers might like to share.

"Well, I'll be damned," said Buck.

"Coyoons, eh?" said Shady.

"Sounds like Uncle Bub might have had a couple of extra cups of mocha java before he wrote that column," said the poet Vance Lancet.

Vance had taken a strong dislike to Uncle Bub while working off the terms of his probation in the Crustacean Liberation Army incident as a volunteer aide for Uncle Bub's Buddies.

"You can laugh, but I've heard of coyoons before," said Buck

Aroux. "We call them 'loupettes' up in Canada, little wolves that wear masks. I'm sure Uncle Bub knows what he's talking about."

"Well, I've never seen one before," said Shady.

The breakfast discussion was cut short as Buck and Shady were dispatched to Chesterville where a lady had reported that two moose were eating their way across her backyard.

But the next morning, back at the Chicken Coop, there was plenty to talk about concerning coyoons, because not only had Uncle Bub written another column about them, but also another one had been sighted the previous day.

Two elderly ladies in New Peru had gone down to pick fiddleheads when they spotted what they told the sheriff's office looked like two dogs. These critters had given the two ladies quite a fright and badly scared them so that they dropped the fiddleheads and ran all the way back home screaming.

Buck and Shady studied the account of the coyoon sighting in the morning paper, complete with a photograph showing both women standing in their kitchen with shotguns at the ready and the caption, "Coyoons give a fright in New Peru."

> Lucille Butterworth and her sister, Massie, are shown here in the kitchen of their home in New Peru, at the ready to defend themselves from a pack of coyoons believed to be in the area. The Butterworth sisters were on their way home from gathering fiddleheads when they spotted the predators. Both women received quite a fright, although neither was injured. "Those coyoons better watch their step or they'll get a double-barrel welcome or my name isn't Lucille Butterworth," Miss Butterworth told the *Post*.

"Well, imagine that, two coyoons right here," said Buck.

"They'll be seeing them from Fillmore to the Canadian line now," said Shady.

About this time Buster and Junior Flagg stopped in for a cup of coffee and reported that they had just run into Chick Devine down at the *Clarion* office where he was taking out an ad.

"Chick Devine is offering big money for someone to capture a coyoon alive," Buster said.

"Is that a fact," said Shady.

"Five hundred dollars and a lifetime pass to the Fun O'Rama," said Junior.

"We're thinking about trying to do it," said Buster.

"What's he want a coyoon for, the Fun O'Rama?" asked Buck.

"Sure, but he told us he also wanted to start a coyoon breeding ranch and sell the fur," said Junior.

19

Coyoon fever grips a terrified citizenry, and a special task force sets out to capture the wily beast.

For the next week hardly a day passed without another sighting of a coyoon, and as the days passed, the number of sightings increased. Every morning there was another account of a coyoon or a pack of coyoons or a pair of coyoons running around someplace in Maine and giving people a hell of a scare.

A pack of coyoons blocked the runway at Captain Emile LaFleur International Airport in Abenaki County one morning, causing the Abenaki Airlines shuttle, which linked Fillmore with the outside world, to be briefly diverted to Augusta.

Junior and Buster Flagg, who were engaged as skycaps at the airport, were sent onto the runway to bang garbage-can lids together to frighten off any coyoons that might be lurking nearby and to allow the Abenaki Airlines shuttle to land safely.

The pilot of the craft, Raymond "Big Ray" Fredette, a veteran of World War II and a famed crop duster who occasionally worked in air shows as a stunt flyer, vowed not to let the roving coyoons interfere with interstate commerce again.

The next morning Big Ray had outfitted his aircraft with what he termed was "sufficient firepower to repel the enemy." Big Ray was accompanied on his flight by the eagle-eyed Armand "Flash" Paradise, serving in the capacity of tail gunner.

Within two weeks of the first report of the coyoon epidemic in the column written by Uncle Bub Varney, there were sightings far too numerous to keep track of. The state then set up a special command post at Red's Gas-N-Go with a toll-free number for residents to report coyoon sightings.

Buck and Shady were about this time named to head a special task force to study the coyoon problem.

A chicken farmer near Union reported that two coyoons had killed and partially eaten an estimated 120,000 chickens during the night and then gotten into the garbage and made, in his words, "a Godawful mess."

Meanwhile, sanitary landfills in some three dozen communities had asked for armed assistance from the state because of concern over daytime coyoon raids.

Off-duty state troopers were assigned to ride shotgun on garbage trucks in many communities, and motorists were warned that littering from their cars was not only illegal but also could be hazardous.

With all of the talk about coyoons around Maine, including a sighting right across the street from Blaine House, the governor's official mansion in Augusta, nerves were on edge.

Governor Harland Payson Getchell ordered the coyoon task force assembled to immediately come up with some proposals on how to deal with the threat.

In addition to Buck and Shady, Uncle Bub Varney was also named to the committee, along with Farlin Dow, Cliff Leach and the poet Vance Lancet.

The problem with the coyoon crisis at that point was that although a vast army of coyoons had been seen from one end of Maine to the other, and sightings were increasing at the astonishing rate of one hundred per day, no one had actually captured, shot or even photographed a coyoon.

The figures kept coming into the special coyoon command post, and by the end of the third week of the coyoon watch, officials estimated that for every citizen in Maine there were at least four coyoons out there somewhere.

The crafty coyoons were not to be trifled with, for as soon as a posse of nimrods was assembled to track them down, they were off, and the pursuers invariably returned coyoonless.

The coyoon posses did not always return completely empty-handed from their forays against the vicious predator. More than two hundred stray dogs were captured, along with a large selection of farm animals, and the holding pen out behind the warden station in Fillmore was full.

One morning, a few days after Governor Getchell issued his instructions to the coyoon task force, the members of the committee met at the Abenaki County Courthouse to plan a strategy to deal with the coyoon menace.

In addition to the committee members, Judge Rufus T. Spurgeon, who happened to be in the courthouse where the meeting was held, attached himself to the deliberations.

Opinion on the coyoon crisis was divided into three camps.

Uncle Bub and Farlin Dow, who were joined by Judge Spurgeon, who admired men of action whenever he encountered them, held that a massive armed effort was necessary to eradicate coyoons and insure the safety of generations unborn. Uncle Bub and Farlin Dow were eager to lead this campaign.

Another position, favored by Cliff Leach and the poet Vance Lancet, held that these creatures needed to be protected and that more research was necessary. Cliff and Vance were hoping to get a grant for further study.

Buck and Shady held the third opinion, as they were unconvinced that there were any coyoons since they had not seen one and no one had even been able to photograph a coyoon, either.

A photograph in the *Abenaki Clarion* purporting to show two coyoons actually showed Victor Fontaine's watchdogs and was sold to the newspaper by pranksters.

As no clear majority position could be arrived at, and with all parties opposed to compromise, Buck and Shady decided that a coyoon, even just one coyoon, must be captured.

"If they exist," Shady said.

Chick Devine's offer of a coyoon reward, increased now to a thousand dollars, had sweetened the pot, and the philanthropic Chicker had also agreed to underwrite the cost of the entire expedition.

A few days later Buck and Shady, along with Uncle Bub and Farlin Dow and a number of others, including Roger Caron, who came along to act as Uncle Bub's gun bearer, assembled up near Bald Pate Notch to flush the elusive coyoon from its lair. The posse reckoned that the cagey coyoon would be most likely found near the source of its first sighting.

Raymond "Big Ray" Fredette and tail gunner Armand "Flash" Paradise were engaged to fly air reconnaissance over the search site.

Farlin Dow, fresh from cataract surgery and raring to go, was placed in his wheelchair at the head of the paper company's road to act as a spotter if any of the coyoons made a mad dash across the roadway while the beaters—Wayne, Duane and Victor Fontaine and Buster and Junior Flagg—were in the brush.

Uncle Bub, using a rarely seen coyoon call, positioned himself about three miles down the road in a blind with Buck, Shady and gun bearer Roger Caron.

Cliff Leach and the poet Vance Lancet, wearing white arm bands and carrying a Swiss flag, stationed themselves nearby to act as neutral observers and insure that the rights of the coyoon were protected when it was taken into custody.

The first morning proved uneventful, as no coyoons were sighted and the beaters complained unceasingly of the ferocity of the deerflies in the woods. This situation was remedied with the distribution of a special repellent, Uncle Bub's Fly Balm, a locally marketed tincture designed to protect hunters and hikers from insect pests.

"Don't smoke while you got that stuff on you," Shady warned the beaters.

Farlin Dow did get off a few shots during the opening hours of the search, once narrowly missing Buster Flagg.

The quest was halted for lunch, and members of the posse avowed that the cunning beast was not to be easily had.

The afternoon proved even more uneventful with no further luck, although Uncle Bub's proficiency in the use of the coyoon call brought a number of beagles and other dogs of the hunting variety down to the search site.

Several curious cows pastured nearby also wandered over on hearing the call of the coyoon. The mooings of these critters further hampered the search and raised questions about their immediate safety, as Farlin Dow was a mere two hundred feet from where they were grazing.

Fortunately for the cows, as well as for the beaters, Farlin Dow had gone into a deep sleep following his lunch and remained so disposed through the entire afternoon.

The second day proved more exciting, due in part to the decision by Buck and Shady to have a coyoon trap dug, a large camouflaged pit.

This was agreed upon by all members of the posse after some debate but thought to be the most environmentally sound method of trapping a coyoon without harming it. However, Cliff Leach expressed some concern that the coyoon could be injured or traumatized by the fall into the coyoon trap.

So several large mattresses were hauled up from town on loan from Jerry's Liquidation City and Carpet Kingdom and placed in the bottom of the coyoon pit to cushion the creature's arrival in custody.

A full morning of Uncle Bub's blasts on the coyoon call and numerous sweeps by the beaters failed to attract a single coyoon.

Buster and Junior did, however, flush out a lone skunk who proceeded to make his opprobrious fragrance known to the posse, particularly the stationary Farlin Dow, who was given a thorough blast, requiring his withdrawal from the search and return to town for a dip in a vat of tomato juice.

Farlin Dow's personal effects required immediate burial, and he was put straight to bed by Darlene Varney after his encounter with the pungent polecat.

The afternoon's pursuance of the irascible coyoon was also without success, due partly to the disappearance of Victor, Wayne and Duane Fontaine, who were believed to have quit the field and gone to town.

But at day's end, examination of the coyoon pit revealed the Fontaine brothers resting peacefully on the mattresses at the bottom of the coyoon trap. A lengthy extension ladder was required to extricate the trio from the pit.

The members of the posse then returned to the county seat to comfort their fallen comrade Farlin Dow, and to reconnoiter as to whether this futile effort was to continue.

As it turned out, Chick Devine, as underwriter of the expedition, put a stop to things, citing increasing costs and complaining bitterly about the purchase of sixty gallons of tomato juice.

No coyoons were captured, but something did come of the expedition. Jerry Velure offered the mattresses used in the coyoon trap as part of his Coyoon Days Sale at Jerry's Liquidation City and Carpet Kingdom.

20 ▲ ▲ ▲ ▲ ▲ ▲ ▲ ▲ ▲

In which plans begin for the Maine Event, a celebration of real Maine life.

Perhaps modesty was Chick Devine's greatest frailty, and so it is that we shall never actually know how it was that the impresario came up with the idea to hold a festival to celebrate the real Maine.

In an interview with the *Abenaki Clarion*, Devine said that the idea of celebrating the purity of Maine life came to him while he was acting as a judge at the Maine State Speech Contest, where annually the cream of the state's high-school scholars were required to wrestle with the age-old question, "What is the real Maine?"

As usual, Chick Devine was serving as chief judge of these forensics and was ably assisted by a panel erudite enough to pass judgment on such a weighty matter. These included the poet Vance Lancet, Judge Rufus T. Spurgeon and State Representative Jerome B. "Jerry" Velure.

It was not long after the contest that visitors to Chick Devine's office at the Fun O'Rama's winter headquarters in Fillmore were to spy the busy Chicker on the telephone, drumming up support for the Maine Event, or so he was to call it.

Judge Spurgeon was appointed to head a panel to review quality control so that only the purest examples of Maine life, real Maine life, would be allowed to be exhibited at the festival. The learned judge was assisted in his deliberation by what Chick Devine termed "our panel of experts on Maine life," and included, in addition to his speech contest cohorts, Charmaine McCrillis Dinsmore, the heiress and thespian; Gorham "Bub" Varney, outdoorsman, journalist and foe of the coyoon; the ancient nimrod Farlin Dow; and Professor H. Leopold Berlitz, interdisciplinarian and man about the arts.

"We must have rules," Judge Spurgeon cautioned his copanelists. "We must have regulations. Otherwise all sorts of pretenders, poseurs, frauds, phonies, false prophets, fakers, philistines and fly-by-nighters will be upon us."

"A sound idea, counselor," said Chick Devine.

Among the first applicants to present himself to set up an exhibition at the Maine Event was Assistant Warden Lucien "Buck" Aroux, who in his free time operated Aroux's Trailer Heaven.

As Buck's was the finest trailer park in the State of Maine and for many years the official Maine State Trailer Park, the members of the quality control review board agreed unanimously and with little discussion that Aroux's proposal to construct a temporary trailer park exhibition at the Maine Event was well within the bounds of the spirit of the gala.

"This will give visitors a chance to view the real Mainers making their homes and going about their simple and traditional daily lives," said Judge Spurgeon.

"Why not an entire model Maine community—a Maine town in scale-model reproduction for all to see?" Chick Devine asked the august panel.

After some debate the panel of experts agreed that such a

concept could be included in the Maine Event despite space considerations.

"But we must limit this to institutions that all Mainers will be familiar with, representations of the good Maine life familiar to one and all from Madawaska to Monhegan Island," said Judge Spurgeon.

"What things come to mind when you think of a typical Maine town?" Chick Devine asked the experts.

"The village green and the railroad station," said Farlin Dow.

"Right you are," said Chick Devine. "But what has happened to most village greens and railroad stations?"

"There aren't any passenger trains left in Maine," said Judge Spurgeon.

"Correct."

"The village green has been paved for parking in most places," said Uncle Bub.

"Right again. So in our model community we pave the village green and turn the railroad station into a Laundromat," said Chick Devine.

"Splendid," said the judge.

"Okay, now, let's not stop here," said Chick Devine.

"What else should be included?" asked Charmaine McCrillis Dinsmore.

"Don't forget the liquor store," said Uncle Bub.

"Another nail hit squarely on the head," said Chick Devine.

"But we can't put a liquor store right on Main Street in our model Maine community," said Judge Spurgeon.

"Right again," said Chick Devine. "We'll have to hide it. We don't want people to know we drink."

"What else?" asked Charmaine McCrillis Dinsmore.

"Come on now, the rest of you, don't let Farlin and Uncle Bub and the judge do all the work," said Chick Devine.

"I suppose we should have a vet's club, like the Rosaire J. Marcoux Post of the Veterans of Foreign Wars," said Lee Berlitz.

"And what about churches and schools?" said Charmaine.

"You're missing the obvious stuff. Think about this now. What do most towns in Maine have in their business districts?" asked Chick Devine.

"Stores that are closed," said Lee Berlitz.

"Good. So what we need are a block or two of stores that have gone out of business."

"Don't forget to soap the windows," said Farlin Dow.

"An important touch, Farlin. Nice detail," said Chick Devine.

"What will we call our Maine community?" asked Charmaine.

"A good question," said Chick Devine. "This town definitely needs a name."

"What about an Indian name?" asked Uncle Bub.

"That wouldn't be a bad idea," said Chick Devine.

"I favor a traditional Maine name," said Farlin Dow.

"For instance?" said Chick Devine.

"What about Dow's Landing or Dowville?"

"I'm not sure about that," said Chick Devine.

"Dow Plantation?" said Farlin Dow.

"No, no way," said Chick Devine.

"Dow Corners?"

"Sorry."

"Dowburgh? Dow City? Dow Acres? Dow Falls? Dowford? Dowland? Dow Pond? Dow Lake? Dowport? East Dow? West Dow? North Dow? South Dow? Old Dow? Dowborough? Dowfield? Dow Hill? New Dow? Dow Gore? Dowbury?"

"No, no."

"Wait, wait. I'll think of something," said Farlin Dow. "I've always wanted something named after me."

"What about something from the Bible?" said Charmaine.

"Why, of course," said Chick Devine.

"Nazareth?" said Uncle Bub.

"Jerusalem?" said Farlin Dow.

"No, we need something uncommon, something a little out of the ordinary," said Chick Devine.

"Sodom?" said Uncle Bub.

"Gomorrah?" said Farlin Dow.

"Bad for our image," said Chick Devine.

"Gehenna?" said Lee Berlitz.

"That's got a nice ring to it," said Chick Devine.

"Make that New Gehenna," added Lee Berlitz.

"Why, that's just great, sounds like a real Maine town. New Gehenna, Maine, a model community, a great place to work, play and pray," said Chick Devine.

"What's next?" asked Judge Spurgeon.

"Well, we have to talk about the special quality of life in New Gehenna," said Chick Devine.

"No zoning," said Farlin Dow.

"Absolutely," said Chick Devine.

"A real Maine town," said Uncle Bub.

"Can something be named after me?" asked Farlin Dow.

"Not to worry, Farlin. We're naming the sanitary landfill after you," said Chick Devine.

"This is a hell of an idea," said Lee Berlitz.

"We've got ourselves a real slice of Maine life here," said Chick Devine.

"Wait a minute," said Jerry Velure. "Let's take a look at this thing. We've got a model Maine community. But all we have are stores that are closed, a paved-over village green, a railroad station that's been turned into a Laundromat, a liquor store and a big trailer park. There's something missing."

"I know what you're driving at. And I already thought of it," said Chick Devine.

"You have?" said Jerry Velure.

"Just outside of our model community we'll have a shopping

center. The New Gehenna Mini Mall. Everything will be out there, just like in the real Maine."

"Isn't there anything else we want in our model town?" asked Charmaine.

"Factory outlets," said Uncle Bub.

"A stroke of genius, Bub," said Chick Devine. "Now you're talking Maine Event."

21 ▲ ▲ ▲ ▲ ▲ ▲ ▲ ▲ ▲

A dispatch from the professor to Chick Devine concerning mat-
ters vegetarian. Lee Berlitz makes his own special suggestions
for the Big Event.

Dear Chick,

Here I am settling down in the old married life. We are
now living in the cottage behind the Cape Squab Dinner
Theater, which will be opening next season in an effort
to bring fine theater to the people of this deserving state.

As much as I am tempted by your offer, I don't think
we will be doing a revival of *The Boys in the Bateaux.* I'll
be the first to admit that it's a crowd pleaser.

But we are catering to a more sophisticated element here
on Cape Squab, particularly the folks over at Pomona, the
artists' retreat. And they demand more thoughtful productions.

So as you may have already guessed, I am writing one
up right now and I'm up to my elbows in another historical play for Charmaine. I'm trying to cover all my bases
here and also showcase Charmaine's very considerable tal-
ents and work in her late great-aunt's poesy too. No small
feat, even for an old showman.

As you may have heard, Charmaine's one-woman reading of the poetry of Lillian McCrillis Sangerville was a great success. I called it, *An Evening With Lillian McCrillis Sangerville.*

Granted, we had a modest turnout, and while I think of it, I'd like you to thank the Havana brothers for driving all the way down here to be with us on opening night. I'm not sure that those little chimps that they bring everywhere with them really are able to appreciate an evening of poetry, but they were well behaved.

My latest historical opus will also focus on Lillian McCrillis Sangerville's life. How's *The Millionairess and the Muse?* Just an idea. Of course, Charmaine will play the lead.

Jerry Velure is still working on having a rest area named after the old girl on the interstate. It's the only piece of legislation he is introducing this session, so he says he thinks it ought to pass.

Judge Spurgeon is also working on this and plans to make a spirited presentation down in Augusta when they have a public hearing. I know you'll want to be on hand too.

We plan to use the proceeds from this next extravaganza to help restore Forsythia Lodge. As you know, much of the property nearby has been sold off, and we hope to make enough money to buy back a bit of it and move that Laundromat out of there. I can't tell you how it breaks Charmaine's heart to see that across the street from her great-aunt's home.

The real point of my writing to you is that a couple of former colleagues of mine from my academic days are now up here in Maine teaching at the University of Maine's mobile campus. They're going to be up at Abenaki State Teacher's College as guest lecturers soon, and I thought you might want to nail them down for the Maine Event.

Maxwell Tuber and Jean Claude Humus are part of the new macrointerdisciplinary studies program.

Tuber is a vegetarian poet, philosopher and historian, actually a revisionist vegetarian historian. He's working on a grand scale at the moment to rewrite the history of Maine from the viewpoint of vegetables, which he believes are the state's forgotten residents.

You may be familiar with his critical works, often quoted by Cliff Leach on *The Garden of the Airwaves*. Tuber wrote *Organic Anapest Control, Dactyls and Trochees in Your Garden* and *Coping With Catalexis*.

Humus is a vegetarian filmmaker. You may have seen some of his stuff on public television. But I think you will find that he has moved away from some of his earlier work, like *Spuds*, a working-class vegetable documentary about vegetables coming of age in the 1930s.

He has also come a long way from that period when he made *The Corn Bores*, which was very broad vegetable slapstick comedy, or *Herb and Spicy*, a warm if somewhat maudlin tale of two vegetables in the Navy.

A lot of this stuff was part of an attempt by Humus to deal with that special relationship between male vegetables.

Probably his best-known work outside of this country was the brilliant, but controversial, *Les Aphids*, which was really the first vegetable film noir. This film made Humus in his native France but was attacked by the popular press here as too highbrowed.

Humus is making a documentary now about Tuber's work. He'll be filming Tuber while Tuber rewrites the history of Maine from the vegetable perspective and travels around the state conducting interviews with old vegetables. All of this will be intercut with actual footage of late-nineteenth- and early-twentieth-century vegetables.

Now here's where it gets interesting. Tuber is also writing the first critical evaluation of the films of Humus. So we have a filmmaker making a documentary film about a film critic writing a book about the filmmaker. I think

I've got that straight. That ought to take the wind out of their sails down at Pomona.

This project is being funded by the federal government with a matching grant from Title 99, the Vegetable Repatriation Act. As you probably know, the funding was originally earmarked to send displaced vegetables back to their native soil. The federal judge who ruled in this case ordered the states to begin repatriating all vegetables who wished to return to their ancestral homes. In subsequent rulings, as the litigation has expanded, additional funds have been set aside to do all kinds of things for vegetables.

Until I met up with Tuber and Humus I had no idea that there was such funding available for projects relating to vegetables. According to Tuber, he was one of the original members of the team that produced *Why Johnny Can't Eat Vegetables* and *A Special Place for Vegetables*. This is just the beginning.

In addition to the federal government, there are a number of private foundations and special-interest groups with plenty of capital they are eager to spend on just about anything connected with vegetables.

Charmaine and I have a grant application filed with the Greenhouse Foundation in Washington, D.C., which I think might interest you. They are interested in someone writing and producing an original dramatic work or works about vegetables, which brings us back to the subject of our upcoming summer season.

The vegetarian puppeteers Octa and Terza Rima, who run the improvisational vegetable street theater in Cambridge, the Biodegradable Ensemble, have agreed to come here to Cape Squab for the summer.

I am also trying to encourage some of the more diverse groups, such as Rind, the militant lesbian vegetable mimes, as well as the Husk Family, the vegetable commune that collects oral vegetable history.

I have told Humus and Tuber to look you up. I think they are definitely candidates for the Maine Event. Thinking of you and show business.

Your pal,
Lee

22 ▲ ▲ ▲ ▲ ▲ ▲ ▲ ▲ ▲ ▲

*In which we learn more about the Maine Event and something
of Chick Devine's philosophy about Vacationland.*

In ADDITION to Chick Devine's Fun O'Rama, a mainstay of
the festival, a number of local residents wished to offer family-
style entertainment during the Maine Event. But to insure that
only the highest standards were maintained and that safety came
first, as Chick Devine would say, another panel of family-fun
experts was set up to screen the applicants.

Along with Chick Devine and Lee Berlitz, it included the
former Flying Disc operator and marine biologist Roger Caron,
Cherry St. John and Moe Havana.

A fierce debate broke out almost immediately over an application to give pony rides and traditional Maine hayrides.

"Extremely dangerous," said Chick Devine.

"Ponies are very unpredictable," said Lee Berlitz.

"I once knew a girl who worked with a pony," said Cherry.

"What about rabies?" asked Roger Caron.

"What about dangerous ticks hiding in the hay? What if they
bite some unsuspecting fun-seekers?" asked Chick Devine.

"Hay is flammable. We can hardly take the chance," said Moe
Havana.

"I think I've heard enough," said Chick Devine. "These people must have no regard for life and limb. Imagine them wanting to expose Maine Event-goers to something like that."

The matter was tabled for further study by another panel.

Meanwhile the committee approved an application by Victor, Duane and Wayne Fontaine to operate Fontaine's Hell Cars, a stock-car ride that the brothers Fontaine assured the panel would "please the whole family."

Raymond "Big Ray" Fredette was also given a permit to operate Big Ray's Air Show, with the proviso that small children, heart patients and the elderly would not be taken aloft.

"Make sure they sign that waiver, pal," Chick Devine cautioned Big Ray. "Once they sign the waiver, bombs away."

As part of the air show, Armand "Flash" Paradise was to stand on the wing of Big Ray's aircraft and swallow live smelts while Big Ray buzzed the field.

"A crowd pleaser if I do say so myself," said Chick Devine.

"Isn't that a bit dangerous?" asked Jerry Velure, who was sitting in on the deliberations.

"No more dangerous than driving your own car," said Chick Devine. "People get killed every day, you know, just going down to get a quart of milk."

"Sure, but they don't go down to get a quart of milk while standing on the wing of a moving plane trying to swallow live smelts, especially a plane flown by that crop duster," said Jerry Velure.

Chick Devine fixed his gaze on Representative Jerry Velure.

"My dear man, I know that as one of Maine's solons you have a special duty to see to the general welfare of the citizenry. But I assure you, there is nothing dangerous about standing on the wing of a moving plane and swallowing live smelts. Safe as being home in bed, right, Roger?"

"Well, I don't know about that," said Roger.

"In any event, I give you my solemn oath as an entertainer of long standing and as a gentleman of the old school that what Mr. Raymond Fredette and his associate Mr. Armand Paradise propose to do is just as safe as going down to the corner to get a quart of milk."

"But you said people get killed going down to get a quart of milk every day," said Roger Caron.

"Did I say that? You must have misunderstood me," said Chick Devine.

"Look, this is fine by me. As long as we have no legal responsibility for any of this stuff," said Jerry Velure.

"We're in the clear," said Chick Devine.

"Fine, so what else are we offering in the way of entertainment?" asked Jerry Velure.

"Roger will be at the controls of the Flying Disc, offering brave souls an experience unlike any other," said Chick Devine.

"Flying Disc?" said Jerry Velure. "You know, I seem to remember something not so long ago about a Flying Disc. I think it was down on the coast near Rockland. The thing threw a guy across the street and right through the side of a house or some damn thing. It must have killed him. I don't remember the details. This isn't the same thing, is it?" asked Jerry Velure.

"Gracious," said Chick Devine. "You certainly don't think we would allow something like that to go on, do you?"

"Just asking."

"This is a highly sophisticated machine. Why, it was used to train the astronauts if I'm not mistaken. Why, Roger spent a considerable amount of time training to operate this device," added Chick Devine.

"Okay, so what about those Fontaine boys? They're bad news if you want my opinion," said Jerry Velure.

"I beg your pardon?" said Chick Devine.

"I go back a long way with those guys, and I'm not sure that they are the kind of people we want. I was under the impression that they were going to run something like bumper cars, something for kids. I don't like the sound of this Fontaine's Hell Cars one bit."

"Those young men have turned their lives around, and I will be the first to say so," said Chick Devine.

"But isn't it kind of dangerous to allow them to operate a thing like that? I mean, those cars they use will go well over a hundred and forty miles an hour," said Jerry Velure.

"But safety comes first," said Chick Devine.

"What do you mean?" asked Jerry Velure.

"The Fontaines will be driving those cars. Maine Event-goers will be passengers, safely enjoying the thrill of a stock-car race."

"That's what I'm worried about," said Jerry Velure.

"I'm not sure that you have the grasp of fun for the whole family that's necessary to serve on this committee," said Chick Devine.

"Perhaps you're right," said Jerry Velure. "I was really interested in the educational and cultural aspects of the festival, and I plan a big exhibition from Jerry's Liquidation City and Carpet Kingdom."

"Just the thing to set the tone," said Chick Devine. "And may I suggest a display of traditional Maine home furnishings."

"We're going to empty the warehouse," said Jerry Velure. "This will be the biggest cultural and educational display of discount home furnishings ever seen in Maine. And prices will be slashed. I am planning to bus in school kids, senior citizens, shut-ins, at my own expense. We're talking once-in-a-lifetime here, Chick."

"Slashed?" said Chick Devine. "Now you're talking Maine Event."

"I don't want to blow my own horn," said Jerry Velure.

"Don't be shy," said Chick Devine.

"We plan big things for this festival, this Maine Event. I'm a Maine boy, and I want to stand up and say that as a Maine boy I can put together the biggest damn selection of quality home furnishings, appliances and other fine items for the home as could be assembled anyplace in this whole country."

"Don't be modest. Tell the world," said Chick Devine. "That's what the Maine Event is all about. This is our day in the sun."

"Is that right?" asked Roger Caron.

"Damn right it is. We're putting together the biggest collection of the best in Maine life anyone has ever seen on this planet. We aren't settling for second-best or second-rate. We're going first-class all the way on this deal. No ifs, ands or buts about it. First-class all the way. You with me?"

"All the way," said Roger Caron.

"We're putting together a Hall of Culture right now that will dazzle," said Chick Devine.

"Tell me more, I'm all ears," said Jerry Velure.

"Well, if you can keep a secret," said Chick Devine, "this thing is really big."

"You know me, Chick, it's safe with me," said Jerry Velure.

"Promise?" said Chick Devine.

"On my honor as a member of the Maine State Legislature," said Jerry Velure.

"Well, in that case," said Chick Devine.

"Well?" asked Jerry Velure.

"Okay, now keep this under wraps, pal. We're talking the big time here. The really big time. No small stuff here. This is a Chick Devine production unlike anything you've ever dreamed of. I frighten myself sometimes when I think about these things. It may be too big, even for me, but I've got to do it. It's now or never."

"I know you can do it," said Jerry Velure.

"First off, Fontaine's School of Cosmetology will be heading up the list of cultural and educational exhibitors, and Lorraine is doing things in a big way. She plans to have all of her stylists there creating special hairdos for the Maine Event. One to be named after each county in Maine."

"Imagine that," said Roger Caron.

"And Maine Event-goers can, for a small fee, of course, have their own hair styled in the manner of the special coiffures. Now isn't that just what we were talking about? Is that big or what?"

"That's big," said Jerry Velure.

"In addition, Lorraine will have her own group of junior cosmetologists on hand. You know that she's the adviser to the Future Cosmetologists of America up at the regional high school?"

"And what will they be doing?" asked Jerry Velure.

"They're sort of a group of teenage hairstylists and beauticians, a kind of cosmetology drill team, competitive stuff. They call themselves the Cosmettes. It's quite a thing to see," said Chick Devine.

"Sounds like you've got your bases covered," said Jerry Velure.

"Don't stop me now. This is only the beginning, my good man."

"By all means."

Chick Devine took a deep breath and rubbed his hands together.

"Maeve Rideout will be on hand, all during the festival, broadcasting live over WEZY and also advising Maine Event-goers on paracrustaceous problems they may have."

"This woman is the famous paracrustaceous psychologist?" said Jerry Velure.

"The very one, and she'll be available to consider any and all problems that one might have concerning interpersonal relations with mollusks and crustaceans."

"Very educational," said Jerry Velure.

"She'll be alternating with Cliff Leach and Vance Lancet, and they'll be doing a live *Garden of the Airwaves*, helping Maine Event-goers with questions they might have about their gardens."

"Why it sounds like there'll be something for everyone, " said Jerry Velure.

"And there will, my friend. There most certainly will, and you can rest assured about that," said Chick Devine.

"I noticed on the tentative program that there'll be a sightseeing trip to see the foliage," said Jerry Velure.

"Yes, indeed. The leaf peepers. Buster and Junior Flagg will be operating Jack Frost Tours. Their bus will leave the Maine Event site every morning at nine, drive over the Old Covered Bridge in New Peru for photographs, then on to view the foliage and then back in time for lunch," said Chick Devine.

"Foliage?" said Jerry Velure. "Jesus, it's summer. Where the hell are they going to find foliage then? And, by the way, there's no covered bridge in New Peru."

"Look, people come all the way up here to see foliage, there's foliage. What's wrong with you?" asked Chick Devine. "You've got to think big, at least bigger than you're thinking."

"But how are all of these things possible?" asked Jerry Velure.

"The magic of show business, my friend. That's what this is all about. That's what Maine is all about. Give them what they want. They want foliage in July, bring on the foliage. These people expect a covered bridge in every town in Maine, so bring on the covered bridges. Okay, so it used to be a barn. So what's a covered bridge, anyway, just a barn with both ends opened up standing across some running water. Am I right?"

Chick Devine was pacing up and down now, shaking his head.

"Look, people can't be disappointed, otherwise they'll stop coming up here and then where will we be, eh? Up the creek without the proverbial oar. Right?"

"That's paddle, Chick," said Roger Caron.

"You keep your oar out of this, my young friend. "

Chick Devine looked at Jerry Velure and grabbed him by the shoulders.

"No, Jerry, if I may call you Jerry. You have to grab the bull by the tail. This is no country for thinking small, and the Maine Event is not going to think small, my friend. If Maine was a place for thinking small, it would still be part of Massachusetts."

"But some of these ideas are impossible. Look, I don't mean to criticize, but some of this stuff is just plain crazy," said Jerry Velure.

"Impossible," thundered Chick Devine. "Crazy. Chick Devine does not know the meaning of the word *impossible*."

"Well, look at this. Whale watching. We are in Abenaki County, two hours from the coast. How can we possibly take people whale watching? And even if we could, where the hell are we going to find a whale? Jesus, I've lived in Maine all my life and I've never seen a whale."

"Well, you'll be seeing a whale of a whale when the Maine Event is on, my doubting friend. Every day, three shows, with a special matinee for the kiddies on weekends. We've got ourselves a whale, pal, so don't sweat it. I'm talking Moby Dick, Jack. No small whales for Chick Devine. No siree."

Jerry Velure and Roger Caron stared at Chick Devine.

"As a matter of fact," Chick Devine continued, "I'm thinking about whale rides. People will be riding a real honest-to-God whale. They'll be lining up for miles to ride a whale. Hell, that's something you can't do every day. And it beats the hell out of those little ponies, eh? No kid is going to settle for a fifteen-minute ride on some smelly little pony when he can hop into the saddle aboard a whale."

Jerry Velure attempted to speak.

"Don't interrupt me. Plus, we've got the rabies problem licked too. And no biting. Ponies bite, whales don't. Oh, I know they've been known to swallow somebody once in a while, but I think that's probably fairly rare. Of course, we'll take precautions against our whale gulping down a fun-seeker. I plan to have Buster and Junior keep a length of rope handy in case we have to go down inside the whale to retrieve somebody. Jerry, these whale rides could be really big. And it would be a hell of a way to cool off, eh? Ride the whale, yahoo."

"I don't know, Chick, I mean, you know your business, but this whole thing might be getting out of hand. I just don't know," said Jerry Velure.

"You just don't know. That's the problem, Jerry. You can't see the forest for the trees. You've got to have vision, that's what it takes. Maine is many things to many people, and we must never forget that. Maine is a dream, my friend, an illusion, a myth, a fairyland. It exists in the minds of millions, and if we don't remember that, we're sunk. And we are the guardians of that dream, the protectors of that fantasy. Why, Maine is like Shangri-La. It's kind of like a place for children, don't you see? People come up here with all kinds of expectations and hopes, and of course they're unreasonable. But if we let those people down, why, Jerry, we're letting Maine down. Do you want to let Maine down?"

"No, Chick, of course not."

"No, of course not. You don't want to let Maine down. And you don't want to let all of those people down. That's what the Maine Event is all about. We're in the business of not letting people down. Are you with me or not?"

Chick Devine paused and wiped his sunglasses.

"Jerry, one man's Maine is another man's whale ride. That's the point of the thing. Each visitor to Vacationland comes pure of heart and eager to savor our way of life. Each and every man, woman and child has his or her dream about what Maine is and about life here. And that's a very special thing, Jerry. But it's a very fragile thing. Okay, so they're dreaming. Is it against the law to dream? No, it's not. But it ought to be against the law to wake the dreamers. Don't do it, Jerry. Don't wake the dreamers. Let them have foliage in summer. Let them have ice fishing in summer. I'm working on that one. Let them dream, Jerry. Don't spoil it."

Jerry Velure and Roger Caron sat speechless, staring at Chick Devine as he paced back and forth, waving his arms.

"Don't ever forget, they all want something different, and every mother's son of them thinks that his Maine is the real Maine. Each dreamer believes his dream is real, and that's where we come in. We provide real Maines for vacationers, the dreamers. Okay, so there are no whales in Abenaki County, so we're two hours away from the coast. Fine. But you tell those tired people who've driven all night to get up here with six screaming children and a half-crazy dog in the back of their station wagon that they've driven all this way and we don't have any whales to watch. You tell them but not me. No way. I won't do it. I'll get a whale for them if I have to dress Roger here up as one. Not that that hasn't crossed my mind, Roger."

"Be reasonable, Chick," said Jerry Velure. "Please be reasonable."

"Jerry, I haven't got the time to be reasonable. The world is full of reasonable people, and look at the state of things. What the world needs is more unreasonable people."

"Where are we going to have whale rides?" asked Jerry Velure.

"We've got the reservoir, right here in town, close to the Maine Event site, and that ought to do quite nicely," said Chick Devine. "As a matter of fact, it ought to fill another bill too."

"Do I dare ask?" said Jerry Velure.

"Windjammer cruises," said Chick Devine. "I must go down to the sea again, to the lonely sea and the sky, and all I ask is a tall ship and a star to steer her by. I could go on but I won't."

"Windjammer cruises. Jesus wept. You can't get away with this stuff. People will not put up with it. Even the most naive and gullible out-of-stater will not pay to go looking for whales in the town reservoir, much less to go on windjammer cruises out there. Hell, the reservoir is less than a mile long," said Jerry Velure.

"Yes, that's right. But when I look out at that body of water, I see the seven seas, " said Chick Devine. "I see tall ships and men of iron. Two years before the mast. Anchors aweigh. Pipe all hands. Don't you just love the smell of the salt sea air?"

"This is fresh water, Chick."

"Have you no poetry in your blood, sir?"

"Do you think for one minute that anyone will believe that they are near the ocean?"

"I think we've already taken care of that problem."

"And how's that?"

"Roger has been doing a little trapping over at the landfill."

"Trapping?"

"Sea gulls. We've got nearly two hundred of those saltwater scavengers locked up right now in an abandoned chicken house."

"And you expect this to work because you've got two hundred sea gulls?"

"No, but it will help."

"Sure."

"I expect that the fog machine will do the trick."

"Fog machine?"

"That's right. We've got a fog machine that will make this place look like London. You won't be able to see across the street when Roger gets that sucker cranked up. It's all part of the greater plan, don't you see?" asked Chick Devine.

"I don't dare ask."

"This is only the beginning. The Maine Event is only a preview of coming attractions. This is only the appetizer. We have plans beyond this deal. Big plans. Plans so big, they even scare me."

"Jesus, Chick."

"We're going to make Abenaki County into a four-season resort. We're going to make this place the Disneyland of the Northeast. But it'll be bigger than that. We'll have it all. It'll be bigger than Vegas, bigger than Atlantic City. Skiing, swimming, sailing, tennis, all the major sports. Racing, day and night, horses and dogs. Like it? We'll have an indoor stadium that'll seat a hundred thousand, maybe two. We're going to turn this place into something no one has ever seen before, something no one has ever dreamed of."

"Sounds like it. What about game shows?" Jerry Velure asked.

"Jesus, Jerry, I hadn't thought about that. Now you're talking. Now you're contributing. That's the spirit, Jerry, get with the program. Game shows. Twenty-four hours a day. Perfect when it rains."

"But how can a state as poor as Maine support such things? There are only about one million people up here, and half of them are poor, real poor. They can't afford to go to twenty-four-hour-a-day game shows. I don't think you've got the market for this, frankly."

"Wrong. The locals aren't our target market for this stuff. They're going to be the work force we'll need. There's going to be a lot of cars that'll need parking, a lot of janitors and housekeepers. We'll need thousands of workers at Abenaki Estates. That's just an idea, maybe we'll call it Club Maine. What about Club Abenaki? What about something in a foreign language? Got any ideas? Come on, you were doing fine with the game shows. Keep it up, I think we've got a rally going now, Jerry boy."

"I sort of like Club Maine," said Roger Caron.

"Well, that'll do for a working concept. A concept, just remember. We're talking concepts here. We're still on the drawing board, boys," said Chick Devine.

"I've got to hand it to you, Chick, you've got some imagination," said Jerry Velure. "But the kind of things you're talking about take money, and they also take a hell of a lot of political clout. You've got to be able to make things happen, to pull strings. You know what I mean?"

"That'll be no problem," said Chick Devine.

"You must be kidding," said Jerry Velure.

"Not when you're the governor," said Chick Devine.

"Governor?"

"Your honor. The Honorable Jerome B. Velure, Governor of the State of Maine. I like it. Nice sound, eh? Very distinguished."

"Easy, Chick. What are you talking about?"

"It's all part of the big picture. The total concept. How do you suppose we can get this thing on the fast track without some drag down in Augusta?" asked Chick Devine.

"But Getchell is the governor. He's not even being challenged for reelection this fall."

"He doesn't know this yet," said Chick Devine.

"I can't be governor. I only introduced one piece of legislation last term, the bill to get the rest area named after Charmaine's great-aunt."

"You're a low-profile kind of guy, Jerry."

"Chick."

"First we'll need a scandal, something really sordid. An insult to every man, woman and child in Maine, an all-out frontal assault on the sensibilities of everything that's decent. A really steamy attack on the sanctity of family life. Don't pin me down yet, I'm working on it."

"Keep me out of this."

"There's a change coming. The winds of change. Can't you hear them? Fresh air. A new deal. A brisk, fresh breeze blowing through the statehouse, and that breeze is carrying you to the voters of Maine."

"This is all too much. I just came over here to talk to you about the cultural and educational stuff in the Maine Event.

All I want to do is sell some furniture and you want to make me governor. You know, Chick, there are times when I think that you maybe think too big."

"That's been said before, Jerry."

"I think I'll see you later."

"Don't turn your back on destiny, Jerry. Don't do it. You'll regret it for the rest of your life."

"I don't want to spend the rest of my life in a federal prison."

"Think positive. Just remember that we're going to be launching your candidacy very soon. No advance warning. Thousands. Hundreds of thousands will see and hear you. We'll have the eyes of Maine, perhaps the nation, on us—and it's coming soon."

"When?"

"Why, this is what the Maine Event is all about," said Chick Devine. "We're going to use the Maine Event as your coming-out party. Your debut. After the Maine Event there won't be a man, woman or child north of Portsmouth who hasn't heard about Jerry Velure."

"But the only way to get a name on the ballot now is by petition."

"Each and every registered voter who visits the Maine Event will be given a complimentary door prize. All they have to do is sign a receipt. The receipt will be your petition. See how easy all this is?"

Chick Devine put his arm around Jerry Velure's shoulder.

"Look, let's not sweat the small stuff right now. Think big picture. Think total concept. The small stuff will take care of itself," said Chick Devine.

"So what do we do now?" asked Jerry Velure.

"Why, we've got to get the rest of the Maine Event squared away. There are a lot of interesting and enlightening educational and cultural exhibitions I haven't told you about yet," said Chick Devine.

23 ▲ ▲ ▲ ▲ ▲ ▲ ▲ ▲ ▲

Chick Devine continues to think big as trained coyoons, old salts and Chief Francis F. Francis, aquatic daredevil and grand sagamore of the Abenaki nation, join the show.

A FEW DAYS LATER, against his better judgment, Jerry Velure called around to see the visionary showman again.

"Hey, Jerry. Boy, have I got a surprise for you."

"What now."

"Did I tell you about the trained coyoons yet?"

"I thought that thing had died down."

"Wrong again. We will have for the first time anywhere a family of wily coyoons. Not just a family but a family of wily coyoons performing tricks too. This is a first, if I'm not mistaken."

"How did you pull this off?"

"Pepe."

"Pepe?"

"The man who can work miracles with the canine species."

"What now?"

"Pepe's got Lu Lu, Chi Chi and Pepita going through their paces right now, and they make three of the wiliest-looking coyoons you ever laid eyes on. Ferocious and desperate. It's sort of a coyoon Wild West show, and this is how it works. Cherry St. John, Jo Anne and the Princess are dressed up as Girl Scouts. Like it so far? Now this is sort of like a skit. You with me? So the Girl Scouts are out in the deep woods gathering berries. Right? And all of a sudden *Owoo, owoo.* That's the sound of a wily coyoon. A bloodcurdling howl that puts the little Girl Scouts into a panic. Well, who should come racing onto the stage but Lu Lu, Chi Chi and Pepita—appropriately made up to look like coyoons. So they race around the Girl Scouts, howling and baring their teeth. Make that fangs. Pretty exciting, eh?"

Chick Devine rubbed his hands together and looked directly at Jerry Velure and Roger Caron.

"Suddenly, who comes to the rescue but Pepe, and he'll be wearing an Official Maine Guide Correspondence School uniform. I want to give the guides a plug, as a favor to Buck and Shady, see. So Pepe's got this starter pistol and he fires off a few rounds and then lassos the three wily coyoons and saves the Girl Scouts. Good triumphs over evil and all's right with the world. Am I right?"

Chick Devine stared at Jerry Velure and Roger Caron.

"Well, what do you think?"

"I suppose it's no worse than whale watching or the windjammer cruises," said Jerry Velure.

"Wait till you see the Girl Scout uniforms. Very daring."

"Knowing you and those girls, I could hardly expect anything else."

"Don't get me wrong, Jerry. This is tasteful with a capital *T.* Fun for the whole family. My motto. My code."

"So that's the educational portion of the Maine Event?"

"No, no. That's cultural. Education is even bigger. Buck and Shady are handling education, and they've got a special guest star. This will be another first."

130

"This doesn't have anything to do with that school of theirs?"

"Ranger Lou. The king of the Official Maine Guide Correspondence School graduates plus a special handpicked corps of guides to demonstrate the woodsy skills for one and all. Real Maine guide lore."

"So that's it."

"No way, pal. Just warming up. We've got some genuine artistes and craftspersons, as they say. Top-flight talent. This stuff will bring the house down, and it ought to pull in the highbrows, the lowbrows and the brown-rice eaters too. Don't forget my old amigo, Lee Berlitz, now of the Cape Squab Dinner Theater. Old Lee is bringing up a load of talent the likes of which Abenaki County has never seen. They got some out-of-state artistes doing stuff that will knock the whole town dead."

"Tell me more."

"Ever hear of a couple of guys name of Tuber and Humus? Apparently these guys are the last word in the world of vegetables. Lee's arranged for them to be up here conducting workshops and such during the Maine Event. Just between you and me, pal, we got to keep the concept as broad as possible."

"So what else have you got?"

"I've got an authentic, old time storyteller, a dying art these days in Maine," said Chick Devine.

"Where'd you get him?"

"It's kind of a long story. He was going to be the skipper of the windjammer cruises, but I had to make some changes in that arrangement."

"How's that?"

"Guy's name is Clyde Swan, and can he tell Maine stories. Real tall ones."

"Great."

"He's picture-perfect too. Got a full beard, captain's hat, pipe, high-water boots, just what we need."

"So what's the problem?"

"The old salt has never been to sea. Fact is, he's from out in Ohio. But don't let that worry you one little bit. He'll be just fine. See, he thinks he's been to sea. Isn't that the same thing? He thinks he was the captain of an oceangoing sailing vessel. Hell, to hear him talk you'd swear he was the real thing. He applied to handle the windjammer cruises, that's how I ran across him."

"And?"

"While I was waiting for him to show up I got a call from a doctor down at the brain garage in Augusta. He wanted to warn me that one of their star attractions wanted to be one of mine. Said to use caution in dealing with Captain Clyde Swan."

"He's not dangerous, is he?"

"Absolutely not. He's completely harmless, a little lamb."

"So what's the problem?"

"No real problem. We just can't let him take a hundred-foot sailing vessel out with paying passengers aboard. Too risky. The doctor says Captain Swan doesn't know bow from stern."

"So what about the cruises?"

"For the time being I'm going to let Roger handle the windjammer cruises. The boy has a good head on his shoulders. We'll let Captain Swan go along for the ride and regale our visitors with his tales of life on the high seas."

"Chick, you think of everything."

"Jerry, somebody has to do it."

"So how did Captain Swan get to be in the shape he's in?"

"I think it came from reading too much. He's got a thicker Maine accent than Farlin Dow. Apparently he picked that up listening to recordings."

"Holy smokes."

"How he got up to Maine is anybody's guess. Cops found

him wandering around down on the Portland waterfront one night. They took him back to the station house for safekeeping. Nobody claimed him, so off to Augusta. He's in my custody now.

"You know, Jerry, I'm not displeased one little bit with the way the Maine Event is shaping up. We've got the talent, and more of it is coming in every day. Why, I got a letter this morning confirming another cultural attraction."

"What's that?"

"Chief Francis F. Francis, grand sagamore of the Abenaki nation, has agreed to make a special appearance."

"Where'd you find the Chief?"

"Moe Havana ran into him down in Florida where he was hooked up with some aquatic show. The Chief used to do tricks on water skis, dressed in full battle regalia. Of course, by the time Moe met him he was past his prime. But none of that stuff for the Maine Event. No way. I plan to team the Chief with Princess Sachem for a few traditional dance numbers. Perhaps a little chanting or drum playing. Indian crafts too. Nothing too strenuous. Besides, I think an Indian chief in full battle regalia on water skis would cheapen our show."

"Quite right."

"It adds a dimension we must avoid. By God, I'll say this much. We will have standards. And the noble red man, the first American, will not have to perform aquatic tricks on water skis at the Maine Event. No way."

"Stick by your principles, Chick."

"Damn right."

"Is the Chief really a chief?" asked Jerry Velure.

"As God is my witness. Full-blooded Abenaki, and royalty too."

"Well, that's something."

"He's from Maine. Just happened to be out-of-state when Moe met him."

"Glad to see that we can help a Maine man out," said Jerry Velure.

"We may have a spot for the Chief in the future. Before the Chief was a trick water skier, he used to be a miniature-golf pro."

"No kidding."

"He was on the national tour, as I understand it."

"That's great."

"I'm thinking of offering him the pro's job at Club Maine when we put the eighteen-hole professional miniature golf course in."

"Will he take it?"

"I don't know. The Chief is kind of a funny guy. He's really only coming up here to straighten out some sort of legal problem he has. Wanted my advice about it. I put him in touch with my attorney, Holbrook Currier."

"What's his problem?"

"It has something to do with land. I'll tell you about it sometime. Frankly, the thing is kind of crazy. I told Holbrook to humor him, poor old guy."

24 ▲ ▲ ▲ ▲ ▲ ▲ ▲ ▲ ▲

The Virgin of Lac du Loup, or Chick Devine works in mysterious ways.

TIME MARCHES ON.

On a fine Maine spring morning with a steady rain falling and the temperature in the low forties, Chick Devine was sitting at his desk in the trailer Jerry Velure had loaned as a mobile headquarters for the Maine Event. He was reading the *Abenaki Clarion*.

Periodically Chick Devine would read an item aloud to his companions, Roger Caron and Pepe Baraja.

"Boys, we're in the social notes this week. Yes siree," said Chick Devine, folding the newspaper open to an inside page and pausing to adjust his glasses.

Mrs. Inez Huff had used considerable material on the upcoming Maine Event to fill her weekly column, "Across the Backyard Fence."

Chick Devine read aloud.

> Golly whiskers, but here it is press time and I haven't done a lick of work. Well, first off, the whole county is

a-buzzing with news about the upcoming Maine Event, to be held on the campus of Abenaki State Teacher's College the first week of August.

Our own Chick Devine, showman extraordinaire, has vowed that no stone will go unturned in an attempt to present "the finest in family entertainment." Backyard fence-sitters report that Chick and his crew of helpers are busy as little bees down at the trailer they've set up on the college campus.

We bumped into the genial showman just a few days ago down at the bus station while he was waiting for some of his artistes to arrive from out-of-state points. Mr. Devine took time out from his busy schedule to tell "The Backyard Fence" that he would be personally supervising the entire Maine Event and that there would be "more than a few surprises," to use his words.

The county is fortunate to have a man with his extensive training in the demanding field of family fun to organize such a gala.

And while we're on the subject, Abenakians, hope to see all of you next weekend at Lillian McCrillis Sangerville's homestead, Forsythia Lodge. Big doings up there as part of the special blue-ribbon panel fund-raising fete to help finance the Maine Event.

Chick Devine promises that many headliners from the festival will be on hand to meet and greet Abenakians.

Nearly forgot to mention, Backyarders, that Father Romeo Bissonette is busy planning the annual pilgrimage to the grotto at Lac du Loup. The bus will leave the church here at five in the A.M., sharp, on Saturday. Father Romeo says that lunch will be provided by the Little Sisters of Lac du Loup up at the grotto, but pilgrims should bring something to kneel on. A special mass will be said at the grotto, and relics will be available.

And so it was that this holy news prompted the impresario to take up his pen.

Dear Lee:

The Lord works in mysterious ways and His wonders are many. Since my last dispatch I have been made aware of a curious custom in nearby Quebec that I think has some Maine Event possibilities if it is handled with the good taste and sensitivity that is necessary.

How's the Virgin of Lac du Loup sound to you?

Now, before you rush to judgment on this, I want to take a minute or two to tell you about this special presentation.

You may not know this, but just across the border from Abenaki County there's some sort of shrine—I haven't actually been up there—to the Virgin of Lac du Loup.

My adviser on spiritual matters, Pepe Baraja, a retired Roman Catholic, says that this holy site is wicked popular with the devout. Last year the Little Sisters of Lac du Loup—they have the franchise, as I understand it—reported crowds in excess of 250,000. Nothing to sneeze at there.

According to Pepe, miracles of all kinds take place up there, left and right. Or as Pepe himself put it, "The blind made to see and the deaf they hear and the cripples all jumped up and walked."

When I heard that, I said, "That's enough for me, pilgrim. I'm a believer."

I've had a few feelers out on this venture, trying to get the lay of the land.

As I understand it, the Virgin is also regarded as the patron saint of ice fishermen. That's just a homely little custom, see. Ice fishing is not an officially Vatican-sanctioned event, or so I believe.

Now, here in town we have a priest, Father Romeo Bissonette, who I really don't know too well, as the old boy speaks only French. Apparently Father Romeo has got season tickets up there at the shrine, and he goes up all the time, bringing with him busloads of people who are feeling poorly. As I understand it, there's a few clams to be made in this line of work, but fair is fair, he got there first and I'm not interested in jumping his claim. Besides, this is specialty work, and I don't think a heathen can just stroll on in and grab a piece of the action, no disrespect intended.

I dispatched Pepe and Buck—Buck speaks French—over to see Father Romeo about this matter in the hope that I might get him to see his way clear to working up some sort of mobile shrine for the Maine Event.

Pepe and Buck weren't too enthusiastic, but I had high hopes and you'll see that they paid off.

Father Romeo is no babe in the woods when it comes to doing business. He has agreed to handle the mobile shrine for us, but the old boy is extracting a fairly substantial cut for his services.

Still, I like the sound of those crowds up there at Lac du Loup.

Anyway, it turns out that Father Romeo has ambitions as a country-western singer. You could've knocked me down. Apparently he has always wanted to do this, but when he was a lad, they had a crying need for men of the cloth up in Quebec rather than steel-guitar players.

Now, I know you've heard me say that I would never handle another country-western singer again after the trouble they've caused me in the past, but I am going to break an iron-clad rule and revise Chick Devine's code of family fun just this once.

What it comes down to is that if he doesn't get to sing at the Maine Event, there's going to be no shrine. And the son of a gun says that if we try to cut him out, he'll have the Little Sisters up there at headquarters hold some sort of special service in conjunction with the Maine Event that'll cut our gate in half. I'll wager that this is not Father Romeo's first foray into the world of family fun.

So he's going to sing. And as much as I hated to do this, I let him have half the bingo action. That's no small piece of change, as you well know. Folks call it beano up in these parts, but it's the same thing, a poor man's Reno.

Riotous behavior was prevalent in the hall that night, and although the old judge did his level best to stem the tide of disorder, his voice and gavel finally gave out, and Jerry Velure was brought in to act as a kind of relief moderator.

The polemics raged on until the wee hours, with the bulk of the pyrotechnics involving a claim by Chief Francis F. Francis, the aquatic daredevil and grand sagamore of the miniature golf links, that all of the land in the county in fact belonged to his tribe, which wanted it back posthaste. The motion was the subject of much hooting, and many voters distinguished themselves by giving Indian war cries. The Chief vowed to pursue the issue in court.

Another item on the agenda featured the aged marksman Farlin Dow, who made a spirited cameo appearance at the session and brought the house to its feet by proposing that all the bridges between Maine and New Hampshire be dynamited to keep people out. Alas, Farlin's proposal was ruled out of order.

Having obtained what they came for, Chick Devine and Holbrook Currier attempted to make fast for the rear of the hall, but their way was much impeded by supporters who clapped them on the back, shook their hands and beseeched Devine to give them jobs at Club Maine. The showman was also embraced and kissed by ladies of all ages and was required, as is the custom, to pat more than a few babies on the head.

Outside the hall, Chick Devine and Holbrook Currier paused to adjust their clothing and light cigars.

"Counselor, it baffles me that the good people of Maine can be so enthusiastic in their support of things they do not understand. The same citizens who cheered my little address so warmly will be the first to rise in opposition to simpler matters," Chick Devine told Holbrook Currier.

"I can't explain it, Chick," said the barrister.

"Well, pure democracy is a great thing, I'm sure, but we are getting too old for these outings. I suppose we should both get down on our knees tonight and thank the Good Lord that at least we didn't have to face a zoning commission."

"Amen, Chick. Amen."

28 ▲ ▲ ▲ ▲ ▲ ▲ ▲ ▲ ▲

The die is cast and a paracrustaceous encounter session leads to trouble.

Lᴛᴛʟᴇ ɪꜱ ᴋɴᴏᴡɴ about the science of paracrustaceous psychology, and even less was known when Roger Caron became perhaps Maine's most famous sufferer from the trauma that paracrustaceous psychologists now believe afflicts those who have become deeply attached to a mollusk or crustacean.

Roger Caron was a walking time bomb, and no one even knew this at the time. Chick Devine, Lee Berlitz and Jerry Velure, not to mention the rest of the folks at the Fun O'Rama and the busy citizens of Abenaki County, didn't have a clue that this mild-mannered fellow, who was known chiefly for the unfortunate flight of the involuntary aerialist and his dear departed hundred-pound pet from the briny deep, was suffering greatly from the crippling anxieties, phobias, neuroses and traumas that follow loss or separation from a crustacean and/or mollusk or other member of that salty world.

Skeptics still scoff when paracrustaceous psychologists and their certified lay assistants, paracrustaceous counselors, warn of the dangers and deep-seated mental suffering that envelop the victims of these horrible experiences.

All of the signs were there with Roger Caron, if anyone had bothered to look. A trained paracrustaceous psychologist would have spotted them immediately: the refusal to eat in restaurants serving seafood; the inability to pass by or near a lobster pound; and the irrational fear and distrust of lobstermen and clam diggers.

Roger Caron was a basket case each Friday, and the same was true when he heard that someone was having a big clambake in the neighborhood. The sight of an ALL THE FRIED CLAMS YOU CAN EAT sign was enough to send him back to bed for the rest of the day.

And so it was that Roger Caron and his problems, untreated, turned out to be a problem for others, as we shall learn.

In the end, Chick Devine himself would admit that had he known he would have personally seen to it that Roger was treated at the very best facilities by top paracrustaceous psychologists.

At the very worst moments of Roger's suffering, leading paracrustaceous psychologists and researchers from across the nation and dozens of foreign lands were gathered at the Applied Paracrustaceous Research Laboratory on Cape Squab.

The National Center for Paracrustaceous Phenomena at Ipswich, Massachusetts, was also available to help, operating, as it does, a massive computer bank linking experts globally and dispatching teams of observers worldwide when unexpected events involving crustaceans and their kin take place.

Roger Caron's case—his symptoms and the observations about his condition—could have been fed into the national center's computer as part of the attempt to treat him. Alas, like so many sufferers, Roger Caron's case went sadly untreated and his condition worsened.

He was a critically ill young man suffering from tertiary crustaceous paralysis when he happened to run into Maeve Rideout, the paracrustaceous psychologist who was also serving as a special liaison from the Pine Tree Arts Society to the Maine Event.

A highly trained specialist and experienced observer of paracrustaceous phenomena, Ms. Rideout spotted Roger's condition almost immediately and undertook at her own expense to counsel this troubled youth when it was determined that Fun O'Rama health-insurance benefits would not cover such treatment.

It was during those lengthy sessions when the sufferer is urged to relax and recall the troubling events which led to the problem that young Roger began to tell Ms. Rideout not only about his own problems but also about Chick Devine's grand designs for the Maine Event, Club Maine and Representative Jerry Velure.

And once he got started, the whole story came out. Ms. Rideout just could not take notes fast enough. This in turn led to a visit by the prying paracrustaceologist to the offices of certain investigative and regulatory agencies in Augusta.

And so it was that the die was cast.

29 ▲ ▲ ▲ ▲ ▲ ▲ ▲ ▲ ▲

The Maine Event, a celebration of "real" Maine life.

THE GRAND AND GLORIOUS OCCASION that was to be the first, and, alas, only Maine Event opened on a bright summer's morning. There was joy in the hearts of the Messrs. Devine, Berlitz and Velure as they looked out on the grounds of Abenaki State Teacher's College and saw that it was good.

By dawn's early light Maxwell Tuber and Jean Claude Humus, along with a specially handpicked squadron of devotees from Pomona's vegetarian artists' workshop, had begun to assemble the mighty Vegatron, a massive vegetable-based sculpture celebrating Maine life and its history.

The poet Vance Lancet, manning his own booth, Verse by Vance, was sweating over a ream of vellum with a half-gallon jug of India ink and some two dozen freshly sharpened quills at the ready as he scribbled his way through the short-order poesy—sonnets and sestinas; rondeaux, rondelays and rhymes; dithyrambs and doggerel; lays, lullabys and limericks; idyls and odes; ballads, jingles, haikus, villanelles and alexandrines.

The notice at Verse by Vance proclaimed, NO JOB TOO SMALL and IF YOU DON'T SEE IT, ASK.

The poet also offered to pack his poesy for travelers who wanted to take a fresh batch home with them.

Near at hand, the farmer of the airwaves, Cliff Leach, was furiously dispensing advice on all matters agrarian to troubled passersby and alternately broadcasting the Maine Event live for the home audience.

Next to them, along the giant midway of real Maine life, was Buck Aroux's elaborate salute to the mobile home with exhibitions of mobile homes down through the ages, including a special exhibit on red-letter days in the history of mobile homes, prepared with the assistance of the National Endowment for Mobile Homes and the Mobile Home Hall of Fame.

A wax museum featuring historical figures in the saga of the life of mobile homes down through the years had been assembled nearby.

Buck Aroux and Shady Vermouth, in full dress uniform, were next along the midway, manning their booth celebrating the Official Maine Guide Correspondence School, which featured a slide show on the history of the school and its curriculum, as well as hourly testimony by successful graduates on what the course had meant to them.

On the half hour Ranger Lou and a squad of elite graduates went through their paces, to the amazement and delight of the curious.

Maine Event-goers then had an opportunity to meet Uncle Bub Varney and the celebrated sportsman, Farlin Dow, as they enchanted visitors with their true tales of the deep Maine woods.

Farlin Dow also displayed his legendary marksmanship by shooting cigarettes out of the mouths of volunteers—when such stalwarts could be found lolling on the midway.

"Splendid way to quit smoking," observed Chick Devine to Lee Berlitz as the two impresarios sauntered through the exhibits.

Soon they came to the central bandstand where the musical duties were being shared by Rene LaRocque and his Accordion Rascals; Moe Havana's musical charges, outfitted for this occasion in Official Maine Guide Correspondence School uniforms; and Rambling Romeo Bissonette.

On the far side of the bandstand, Pepe and the Pups, along with the Misses St. John, Flambé and Princess Sachem, re-created their dramatic presentation about those crazed varmints of the deep woods, the wily coyoons.

A barrier of a quarter-mile length of chicken wire and several snow fences had been erected around the coyoons' lair, lest the crazed beasts, smelling the crowd, be driven to attack. Chick Devine had ordered the Havana brothers to loan several skeletons from the former medical school they had purchased, and these were arrayed to discourage foolhardy fun-seekers from attempting to actively participate.

Several former bits of divertissement from the old Fun O'Rama were also in operation, including the fabled Flying Disc with the steady hand and cool head of Roger Caron at the control board.

Chick Devine had also dusted off a few old chestnuts, such as the ever-popular Swedish ring toss and the caged LSD victim, played by young Roger.

The entire backside of the Maine Event grounds was given over to a grand and never before assembled display of quality home furnishings from Jerry's Liquidation City and Carpet Kingdom, including two tractor-trailer loads of fire-damaged footwear just in from a factory disaster.

Manufacturers' representatives from the nation's greatest discount outlets rounded out the tribute to commerce and industry with their wares on display.

The mobile shrine of the Virgin of Lac du Loup, tastefully

constructed on the back of a flatbed truck kindly loaned by Jerry Velure, stood at the far end of the Maine Event grounds on a slight knoll.

From that point the Very Reverend Romeo Bissonette, dressed ornately in elaborate vestments on loan from a Boston theatrical costumer, with miter atop his head, presided as the "exclusive North American representative of the Order of the Virgin of Lac du Loup" when his musical duties as Rambling Romeo permitted.

An extensive display of abandoned wheelchairs, walkers, braces, canes and crutches on the grounds of the mobile shrine urged the faithful to throw themselves on the mercy of the virgin for a small fee.

At the very center of the mighty extravaganza a raised stage provided an area for Charmaine McCrillis Dinsmore's interpretive dance company, along with other performers, such as Jean Claude's girlfriend, Miso, and her vegetable origami.

On the town reservoir, the windjammer *Everett Mudge* was anchored, and visitors were allowed to come aboard for a tour of the vessel and a visit with that venerable old salt from the Buckeye State, Captain Clyde Swan.

Periodically Chief Francis F. Francis, litigant and grand sagamore of the Abenaki nation, would pass along the waterfront behind a speedboat in full tribal regalia, and a great shout would go up from the crowd.

Despite the reservations of Chick Devine and his associates, the Chief had insisted on performing his aquatic bits of derring-do, rotating these with appearances on a nearby miniature golf course where unsuspecting souls were challenged to Beat the Chief.

At the great outdoor bingo or beano emporium, Chick Devine and Father Romeo served, time permitting, as co-masters of ceremony by announcing the proceedings simultaneously in French and English.

A much sought grand prize, five thousand dollars' worth of free services from the renowned Body Shop Institute, had drawn considerable attention from Maine Event-goers.

The institute, the brainchild of Wayne and Victor Fontaine, had pioneered the remodeling and retrofitting of old and abandoned cars so that they could be lived in as small, compact, energy-saving homes, easily moved from place to place. The Fontaine concept had eradicated the unsightly heaps of abandoned cars that had previously littered Maine. The institute operated a twelve-part course, which taught greenhorns how to take a standard full-size American car made before 1974 and turn it into a comfortable home suitable for a family of four.

The amazing success and fine reception received by the institute was apparent from one end of Maine to the next, with hundreds of young families previously unable to afford low-cost housing now happily ensconced in their little four-wheel dream homes, thanks to a modest investment in an acetylene torch and a few hundred dollars' worth of sheet metal.

After wandering wide-eyed through this grand display, hungry Maine Event-goers were then enticed to belly up to the massive array of edibles and potables on hand to succor the famished and thirsty celebrants.

Twenty-six flavors of traditional Maine baked beans were available, along with what was billed as the largest fried-dough booth in the Western Hemisphere.

A mile-long loaf of white bread, the combined efforts of Maine's major bakers, was being sliced up by chainsaw-wielding attendants.

There was an alternative Maine shore dinner featuring variations on the more traditional steamed lobsters and clams, fried clams, barbecued chicken and corn on the cob.

This feast offered instead a shore dinner concocted entirely of tofu—boiled, steamed, fried, baked, broiled, sautéed and barbecued—along with tofu on the cob. And the feast was washed down with a frothy stein or two of ice-cold tofu lager, a beer brewed just for the occasion.

And there was, as Chick Devine would say, much, much more.

30 ▲ ▲ ▲ ▲ ▲ ▲ ▲ ▲ ▲ ▲

The morning after brings disaster.

AND SO, the morning after brings news of the Maine Event in the daily newspapers, but alas, this was not the news that Chick Devine and his associates longed to see.

STATE TO PROBE MAINE EVENT OPERATORS
LAND FRAUD, ELECTIONEERING IMPROPRIETIES
CHARGED

The organizers of the Maine Event, billed as a "celebration of real Maine life," are allegedly behind an elaborate scheme to defraud investors in a four-seasons resort complex in Abenaki County, according to investigators with the state attorney general's office.

A special grand jury will be called to consider the case, authorities said yesterday.

In addition, the state also plans to investigate the fledgling gubernatorial campaign of State Representative Jerome B. "Jerry" Velure, who announced during the opening of the Maine Event that he would mount an independent attempt to unseat Governor Harlan Payson Getchell in November.

The move startled veteran campaign watchers in Augusta as Velure's three terms in the state legislature have been marked by low attendance and the introduction of a single bill, an attempt to name a highway rest area after a former constituent.

Velure is best known as the operator of Jerry's Liquidation City and Carpet Kingdom, a discount furniture house that also sells a variety of damaged merchandise.

In his campaign announcement yesterday, Velure vowed to set Maine on firm footing by running the state the same way he has operated his discount house.

Velure summed up his campaign philosophy for reporters by saying, "We're going to slash prices, everything must go." He declined to elaborate and referred all questions to his special assistant, Chick Devine.

Sources familiar with the case say that Devine, the operator of the Chick Devine Fun O'Rama, a carnival popular in rural Maine, is the mastermind behind a bizarre attempt to put Velure in Augusta.

Sources say Devine is assisted in this by Lee Berlitz, artistic director of The Cape Squab Dinner Theater, and a former faculty member at Abenaki State Teacher's College, whose contract to teach interdisciplinary studies was not renewed.

Authorities say that Devine and his associates have already sold thousands of time shares in an as-yet-to-be-built resort complex tentatively called Club Maine. Law enforcement officials in sixteen other states have asked Maine authorities to investigate the Devine operation following complaints from thousands of consumers.

In addition, state election officials will probe allegedly illegal practices that took place at a recent special town meeting in the Abenaki County seat of Fillmore, in which cash and other gratuities were distributed to voters, and promises of jobs were made.

"These investors were under the impression that Club

Maine actually existed and that they were buying into a going concern," a spokesman for the attorney general's office said.

"There is no Club Maine, and we have every reason to believe that there was never any intention of building such a resort. Our investigators can find only a large sign on the outskirts of Fillmore proclaiming the site of the complex. No one has actually built anything. They don't even own a piece of land."

31 ▲ ▲ ▲ ▲ ▲ ▲ ▲ ▲ ▲

Certain dispatches penned by Mr. Chick Devine,
showman and fugitive, as our tale comes to an end.

D<small>EAR</small> <small>ROGER:</small>

Professor Berlitz and I have been called away on urgent business of a highly confidential nature. In our absence I am placing you in charge of the Fun O'Rama and the Maine Event. I know it's a big job, but I think you're ready for this kind of responsibility.

We may be away for a while, so take care of things and do your best to keep up the spirits of the crew. Refer all matters of payments due and debts outstanding to me, and assure any inquirers that I will personally attend to these matters forthwith on my return. Please exercise extreme caution in your operation of the Flying Disc. I have every confidence in you. Good luck.

Your pal,
Chick Devine

Dear Judge:

By the time you get this, Professor Berlitz and myself will no longer be residing here in the heart of Abenaki

County. I realize that things will probably look bad, but all I can say is, don't believe everything you read in the newspapers.

A gross libel has been perpetrated on your correspondent, and I have instructed Holbrook Currier to prepare for battle. I will personally be directing our defense—and I will also hold a news conference to refute any and all charges and allegations.

I did want to take a moment to thank you personally for your many hours of work and advice. I also want to impose on you to ask that should any of my former associates in the world of family fun require the services of a solicitor, please make yourself available. I know that many of these good people may lack the resources to pay you much, if at all; however, knowing you as a true-blue advocate of fair play and a champion of the right to a fair trial, I feel that you will not let any of these deserving folks down.

As for myself and Professor Berlitz, we have found the situation here a tad turbulent, and although we would both rather remain here and battle fiercely to clear our good names, we do not feel this is the appropriate hour.

Given the scandalous dispatches in this morning's newspaper, I do not feel that we could possibly receive a fair trial hereabouts, perhaps not along the entire Eastern seaboard.

And so it is that we must bid you and your charming wife adieu.

Here's hoping that we will all meet again on a brighter day, perhaps on the grounds of Forsythia Lodge, and there toast our time together. Neither the professor nor myself will ever be able to read the poetry of Lillian McCrillis Sangerville without thinking of you.

Your pal,
Chick Devine

Dear Jerry:

Please make arrangements to have the sign marking the site of the Club Maine complex taken down.

Your pal,
Chick Devine

Dear Lee:

I take pen in hand this morning to write with a heavy heart and my weather eye on the clock, for I must soon make haste. Cruel fate has dealt the old Chicker a bad hand. Certain dispatches in today's newspaper make travel seem more broadening than usual.

By the time you receive this, I am sure you will have been made aware that my good name has been besmirched here and our grand plans for the Club Maine placed in great jeopardy.

As the poet said, on an occasion such as this, every man for himself.

Justice is swift this morning, and my aides inform me that a posse is being formed down at the Abenaki County Correctional Center, charged with the apprehension, dead or alive, of these old bones.

I am also made aware that a group of ruffians, vigilantes and dissatisfied investors plan to take the law into their own hands if they reach me first.

Every effort is being made to see that neither of those scenarios takes place.

As an old confederate of mine, I urge you to seek the higher ground if you have not already done so, as I am not certain how vigorously the statutes will be applied to my confreres.

And so it is that I cannot tarry long here with my quill when there are those abroad who would seek to apply measures of tar and feathers to my person.

I have sent my old retainer Pepe into town to tell the rabble that I am down at Jerry Velure's house. This should serve as an appropriate diversion and an added surprise to Jerry, who is home at this hour and unaware of certain developments. As a co-defendant I fear that our solon will have his hands full when the mob finds him, though I pray that he is captured by the authorities first.

I cannot help but take a moment to reflect fondly on our many years in the old craft, bringing family fun where family fun was most needed, here in the great State o' Maine, and of the many good works we have done. Our many kindnesses and selfless acts seem forgotten now as they prepare the gibbet for yours truly.

My health will not permit an extended stay of incarceration, and although I would rather stand and fight, I will quit the field.

Many of our dear chums in the family-fun business are also preparing to weigh anchor at this hour, fearing that association with me might prove a difficulty.

The Havana brothers, veterans of many campaigns, and their entourage have already broken camp.

My greatest disappointment is that the Club Maine will not bear fruit. I am also saddened that I will not be here to assist Holbrook Currier in his legal battle on behalf of our associate Chief Francis F. Francis, who claims that he is entitled to seventy percent of the land in Maine by virtue of some old treaty. As you know, I was offered the position of tribal press agent and social investment adviser to the Abenaki nation.

I cannot say when or whether we will ever meet again, for these things are not up to us to decide but must be left to a higher power, in this case the district attorney's office.

Still, I want you to know that I will think of you and think of this dear old state. I carry Maine in my heart.

Is it too much to hope that when, in years to come, folks see my faded billboards on the sides of silos, they will think fondly of old Chick Devine and the Fun O'Rama?

And so, as an old showman, I bid you adieu and say perhaps for the last time . . .

Your pal,
Chick Devine

Epilogue ▲ ▲ ▲ ▲ ▲ ▲ ▲ ▲

Some time later. . .

Victor and Wayne Fontaine are back in the business of building birdhouses for the State of Maine's Department of Corrections.

Their sister, Lorraine, continues to operate Fontaine's School of Cosmetology, which now has eleven branches in Maine. Brother Duane is now president of the Maine State Teachers' Association.

Inez Huff still reports on the goings-on in Abenaki County and writes her weekly column in the *Abenaki Clarion*, "Across the Backyard Fence."

Buster and Junior Flagg still have the Star Route mail contract and daily make the trip from Fillmore to the Canadian line.

Maeve Rideout now hosts a nationally syndicated radio talk show on paracrustaceous psychology.

Warden Marlin "Shady" Vermouth is now Dean Emeritus of the Official Maine Guide Correspondence School, which will graduate its one millionth guide this year.

Ranger Lou Apponzio vanished during an outing at a state park in New Jersey. A scholarship at the school has been established in his memory.

Melvin, Morris and Morton Havana and their entourage now operate the House O' Chimps near Fort Myers, Florida.

After winning a talent contest Father Romeo Bissonette left the priesthood to devote himself entirely to his music.

Cliff Leach still hosts *The Garden of the Airwaves*, now broadcast nationwide.

The poet Vance Lancet now owns and operates Vance's Poetry Outlet, a mail-order poetry business based in Abenaki County.

Uncle Bub Varney has been enlisting support for another expedition to find the coyoon. Farlin Dow, now 104, remains an active sportsman.

Pepe Baraja and the pups, Lu Lu, Chi Chi and Pepita, are regular guests on a Saturday morning television program for Hispanic youngsters.

Roger Caron was recently arrested while climbing into an aquarium in California with a hacksaw in his possession.

Buck Aroux has since left the warden service to manage Aroux's Trailer Heaven.

Charmaine McCrillis Dinsmore still operates the Cape Squab Dinner Theater, where this season she will star in a one-woman show based on the life of her great-aunt. A divorce court declared her marriage to Professor Lee Berlitz—also known as Professor H. Leopold Berlitz, a.k.a. Lee Berlin, a.k.a. Leo Berle, a.k.a. Bobby Lee Berler, a.k.a. Dr. Leo Berlin—null and void.

The Honorable Rufus T. Spurgeon represented State Representative Jerome B. "Jerry" Velure at his trial. Jerry Velure will be eligible for parole in 1997.

Last year the United States government settled the largest financial claim of its kind in the nation's history as part of a legal action brought on behalf of the Abenaki Indians by Holbrook Currier.

Lee Berlitz is believed to be living on a Caribbean island

that does not have an extradition treaty with the United States.

Interpol reported last year that several West African governments were offering substantial rewards for the apprehension of an American resort developer traveling on a passport issued to C. Devine.

The assets of Club Maine and the Fun O'Rama were disposed of at a well-attended sheriff's auction at the Abenaki County Courthouse where the *Clarion* reported that a wonderful time was had by all.

We are still negotiating the fine print concerning the relic franchise. I was unaware that this was the big business that it is, but apparently it is.

I'm making the good father a headliner, Rambling Romeo Bissonette, the singing Christian cowboy.

> Hallelujah,
> Your pal,
> Chick Devine

Despite Father Romeo's enthusiasm for the mobile grotto, which he hoped would finance a magnificent beano emporium, the envy of every parish priest from Eastport to Block Island, and his dreams of a late vocation as a country-western crooner, it is true that in these troubled times miracles are hard to come by.

So it was that Chick Devine found it necessary to take matters into his own hands and, in the old Chicker's words, coax the miracle along a bit.

No better place for such an effort than in the pages of the *Abenaki Clarion*, faithful handmaiden of the first amendment and spreader of the news.

The first the county seat knew that Chick Devine was working in mysterious ways was when they picked up a copy of the *Clarion* and saw a photograph of Pepe and Roger on the front page, waving crutches.

The headline read: ONLY WEEKS TO LIVE, LOCAL MEN SNATCHED FROM DEATH'S DOOR.

> Two Abenaki County men, whom physicians had given only a few weeks to live as a result of coyoon bites, say that they have been snatched from the jaws of death by a miracle.
>
> The two men, Pepe Baraja and Roger Caron, credit their miraculous recovery to the intercession of the Virgin of

Lac du Loup, whose shrine is in nearby Quebec.

Their complete recovery from this debilitating illness took place yesterday in front of the *Clarion*'s office in downtown Fillmore.

Passersby were startled when both men, heavily bandaged and on crutches, were healed suddenly. Moments before, the *Clarion* was fortunate to receive an anonymous news tip from a caller who advised, "It looks like a miracle is about to take place outside your office."

A *Clarion* lensman was at the ready and captured this momentous occasion on film for our many readers.

"We've definitely been blessed by a miracle," Señor Baraja told the *Clarion*. "This is the work of the Virgin of Lac du Loup."

"No question about that," added Roger Caron.

Both men are employees of the Chick Devine Fun O'Rama, now headquartered in Fillmore.

Their employer, Chick Devine, responding to the miracle, noted that coincidentally a mobile unit from the shrine of the Virgin of Lac du Loup will be here next month during the Maine Event.

Devine said he felt certain that, in his words, "the Virgin's many loyal fans around these parts won't let her down and will come on out to see the show and bring the whole family. Plenty of free parking, folks."

25 ▲ ▲ ▲ ▲ ▲ ▲ ▲ ▲ ▲

The showman pens a letter to the professor, advising of the
Maine Event and requesting assistance.

As the final weeks of preparation began for the first annual Maine Event, Chick Devine dashed off another dispatch
to his old associate Professor Lee Berlitz, the exiled interdisciplinarian, who was still down at the Cape Squab Dinner
Theater, urging him to make fast to Abenaki County to assist
in the final organization of the great occasion.

> Dear Lee:
>
> As they say up here, "I am some wicked busy" these days
> between running around getting things pulled together for
> the Maine Event and shooting trouble. And I can tell you
> that there's a hell of a lot of trouble to be shot hereabouts.
>
> Fortunately, being the manager that you know I am, I'm
> not one bit shy about delegating authority as long as I know
> that I have a solid core of able-bodied assistants.
>
> In that regard I have assembled a team of seasoned show-
> men of the old school, including our old confederates, the
> Havana brothers, who all asked to be remembered to you.
>
> In addition, Pepe and Roger are serving as my right-hand
> men these days. I have also made Pepe special envoy on

religious matters as I fear that my aggressive management of the miraculous cure still does not set well with Father Romeo.

Speaking of the good shepherd, Father R. has shown himself to have many strengths when it comes to the field of family fun, and he has thrown himself into this production, I hope, not at the expense of his little flock.

Buck and Buster and Junior are hard at the assembly of the mobile grotto.

Jerry Velure, our next governor if I have anything to do with it, has been having his hair styled, a sure sign of higher office, as you know.

For maximum publicity, we're planning on announcing Jerry's candidacy on the opening day of the Maine Event.

That brings me to the reason for this letter. Can you spring yourself free for a few days to get up here and help me draft some position papers for Jerry?

From what I can see so far, Jerry's campaign will have to have some issues, although I'd rather the election focused entirely on personalities.

I've been studying recent electoral success around these parts, and issues have never been an issue. Still, I'd sleep better knowing that we had some position papers. We don't need many, but a few are a must. You can pick any old positions you like. Just be sure that Jerry can understand his own positions.

I don't believe that Jerry's outstanding career in the legislature will be a hindrance to us in the fall. As you know, he only introduced that one bill last session, and I can't for the life of me imagine how naming a rest area after an old lady poet could get us in much trouble.

In my assessment of this campaign as an old showman, I believe that in addition to hairstyling we need a grand gesture. Something that speaks to the people of this fair state.

What do you think of having Jerry walk from one end

of Maine to the next? This seems to have worked well for others.

I'm not sure that Jerry is a vigorous perambulator or that he would go for such a stroll. We'll have to study on this.

By the way, I got my hot little hands on a questionnaire that the Portland papers plan to use to outline a candidate's positions on various issues. And, I also got hold of the answer sheet.

Damn thing is, Lee, we haven't even gotten our candidate elected yet and already I'm being hounded by camp followers of the worst sort, seeking political patronage jobs. Can you believe it? Are there no secrets in this state?

Just yesterday Judge Spurgeon, who is serving as special legal adviser to the Maine Event, jumped me over at the Gas-N-Go and asked point-blank about a shot at the state supreme court.

Shady and Buck want jobs too. Though they both hanker after cabinet posts, they say they'll settle for the co-managers' jobs at the state liquor store in Kittery.

As special gubernatorial assistants, we are going to have to decide who gets the plums and who doesn't. The numero-uno plum being the Club Maine complex, reserved for yours truly.

Uncle Bub and Farlin Dow vow that in short order they will straighten out the Environmental Protection Agency and a few other offices they describe as "pink." I've had some philosophical discussions with them, and their feelings can best be described as, "If it moves, shoot it—if it don't, cut it down."

And that reminds me, we're going to need a lake up at the Club Maine site, and this is going to involve rerouting the Abenaki River just a bit. But that shouldn't be any problem. Jerry says he'll get a bunch of trailers for the people living at the lake site.

Well, you can't make an omelet without breaking a few eggs. Am I right?

The important thing up at the Club Maine site is to have that big sign up.

People driving by are going to want to know where their condominiums are going to be. And on that subject, under the time-sharing plan we talked about, each shareholder will be entitled to one day every year in the rugged outdoors in Maine. These babies are moving like hotcakes.

I'm about ready for another swing through major cities along the East Coast, and I'd like to take you along. I've got the slide show all worked up.

I turned prospective buyers away in droves during my last tour. These people want a slice of the good life, pal. I have a feeling that this is going to be the next big fad in this country, a piece of the action at Club Maine.

Watch out, Atlantic City, Chick Devine is on the move.

So much for the good news, Lee. All is not a bed of roses up here. I'm going to need some help handling that Maeve Rideout woman.

She's gone and got herself named to the Pine Tree Arts Council as a special liaison to the Maine Event. We should have never gotten mixed up with the state in the first place. Bad news all around.

That woman's been sniffing around up here the last few days with Cliff Leach and the poet Vance Lancet. I've stalled them pretty well.

She asks a lot of questions. And she also has a lot of constructive criticism to offer, and there's nothing I hate worse than that. I'm trying to run a show up here, and she wants to discuss the impact of rides like the Flying Disc on the subconscious of small children. I told her the rides will scare the subconscious right out of small children.

She's also not too happy about the giant display of quality home furnishings that Jerry is setting up on the Maine Event grounds or Buck's trailer exhibit. Lee, troubleshooting ain't what it used to be.

Anyhow, I see Charmaine around here every so often,

so why don't you just tear yourself away from the dramatic life and join your lovely bride up here and give an old pal a hand.

Come quickly, as I am much in need of assistance.

Your pal,
Chick Devine

26 ▲ ▲ ▲ ▲ ▲ ▲ ▲ ▲ ▲

We are diverted from our narrative by the occasion of the Fontaine Family Reunion where a wonderful time was had by all.

WITH PLANS for the Maine Event in high gear and work nearly completed on the mobile grotto, Abenakians learned in the next week's edition of the *Clarion* about the annual gala Fontaine Family Reunion.

Across the miles the Fontaine family members trekked this past weekend from near and far to gather for the Fifty-seventh Annual Fontaine Family Reunion at the family homestead at Fontaine Hill Farm.

Hats off to Lorraine Fontaine for her able planning of the gala, and to her assistants JoLene Whitham and Juanita Frappier née Fontaine. A great job, girls, and much appreciated by one and all.

The descendants of Ezra Fontaine, the first white settler in the Abenaki region, were treated to a traditional down-home Maine baked-bean supper with all of the fixings.

A special word of commendation goes to Juanita Frappier for her molded jelly salad in the shape of Fontaine

Hill Farm. I know it broke a lot of hungry hearts when that delicious artwork was served up.

More than two hundred descendants and friends of the Fontaines were in attendance at the homestead, including many honored guests such as Harold Fernald, Chief of Probation and Parole for the State of Maine, and his wife, Zora. The Fernalds drove up from Augusta for the gala to surprise the Fontaine brothers, Victor and Wayne.

Victor and Wayne presented the guests of honor with a lovely birdhouse, a replica of the Maine State Prison in Thomaston where both young men honed their woodworking skills.

Duane Fontaine, general science instructor and varsity wrestling coach at the regional high school, narrated a multimedia slide show on the history of the Fontaine family, which was much enjoyed by one and all.

A prize, a combination hunting-fishing license, was won by Alden Fontaine, formerly of Abenaki County but now residing in Fall River, Massachusetts. He was able to identify the most abandoned cars in the yard.

Musical selections were provided by Larmone Fontaine, organist at the Full Gospel Tabernacle in Raymond.

Chief Petty Officer Chester "Doc" Fontaine received the Traveler Trophy for coming the farthest distance to the reunion from where he is currently aboard the U.S.S. *Margaret Chase Smith* somewhere in the South Pacific.

The Golden Oldster Award went again to Clinton Fontaine, who, at 107 years young, is the senior member of the clan. He was brought to this year's fete by his sons, Elwood and Norwood Fontaine, operators of Fontaine's Rubbish Removal and Light Hauling in Veasy. A special treat, one full year of free service at the Chickadee Family Dental Workshop, operated by cousin E. Lester Fontaine, D.M.D., was presented to Clinton.

A congratulatory telegram from State Representative Jerome B. "Jerry" Velure was read, and all members of the

Fontaine family gathered around Clinton for the annual photo session.

Miss Ramona Fontaine, a sixteen-year-old eighth-grader at the Floyd P. Taylor Academy, was named Miss Fontaine Family Reunion this year. Her crowning was held in conjunction with a lovely baby shower hosted for her by the staff of the Abenaki County Family Planning Center.

The annual scholarship to aid a member of the Fontaine family in his or her pursuit of higher studies this year went to Dexter "Dex" Fontaine, son of Mr. and Mrs. Carlton Fontaine of West Southwest.

Young Dex, a recent graduate of the West Southwest Regional High School, where he served as president of the Future Body Shop Owners of America, plans to use the twenty-five dollars to continue his studies at the Abenaki Regional Vocational–Technical Institute.

A special get-well and thinking-of-you was sent to Miss Daisy Fontaine, now recuperating at Arbor Rest Home and Senior Citizens Day Care Center in Cherry Hill, N.J., after a nasty snowmobile mishap while visiting here in late winter.

Plans are already under way for next year's Fontaine gala, to be hosted by Lloyd and Bunny Fontaine at their camp on Sebago Lake.

This year's fete was presided over by master of ceremonies Mr. Chick Devine.

As the two-day jubilee drew to a close, all members of the Fontaine family joined hands in the friendship circle and agreed that a wonderful time was had by all.

27 ▲ ▲ ▲ ▲ ▲ ▲ ▲ ▲ ▲

Being an account of a riotous evening spent at a town meeting in Abenaki County by the showman Chick Devine and his counsel, Holbrook Currier, in which they observed democracy in action.

THERE IS VERY LITTLE ZONING in the state of Maine, and there is virtually no zoning in Abenaki County. However, Chick Devine's plans involving the property on which Club Maine was to be developed were so "dynamic," as he put it, that a special town meeting was required to approve the extensive changes in land use that were anticipated.

Abenakians, being the broad- and far-thinking folk that they are, would not raise an eyebrow over the odd trailer park: however, changing the course of the county's primary waterway and creating what would then be Maine's second largest lake was another matter.

And as there were a few other issues in Fillmore that required the immediate attention of a concerned citizenry, a special gathering of voters was held, and it was under these circumstances that Chick Devine and his longtime legal adviser, Holbrook Currier, found themselves perched on a couple of wooden folding chairs at the Patrons of Husbandry Hall one night.

The democratic showman had had the vision to station his

associates, young Roger Caron and Pepe Baraja, sans pups, out on the front steps of the hall to pass out free Fun O'Rama passes and some modest cash offerings in hopes of making straight the way of the Club Maine.

This promotional gesture had been heartily endorsed by Holbrook Currier, who believed that certain charitable offerings were required to still a potentially hostile element among the voters.

As was the custom in the county seat, Judge Rufus T. Spurgeon was the moderator of the hostilities, as the old jurist was the most nimble parlimentarian in the shiretown, and expert, as the judge himself would say, at keeping the riff and the raff at bay. He used a series of maneuvers not customarily employed at public gatherings and for which no precedent is stated in *Robert's Rules of Order,* including the use of several members of the Abenaki Regional High School's varsity wrestling team, the Abenaki Matmen, as sergeants-at-arms.

The festivities in question drew an inordinately large crowd of idlers, gas station philosophers, gadflies and wags of all sorts, who descended on the hall in hopes of a bit of sport at the expense of others. Poor television programming that evening assured a goodly turnout, and the fact that the county banned the sale of intoxicating potables on such occasions also helped to swell the ranks of voters.

Prior to the meeting, Chick Devine and Holbrook Currier worked the crowd, as Chick would say, applying various secret handshakes to an assortment of lodge brothers. They had taken pains in advance to outfit themselves with a variety of fraternal organization's rings, tie clasps, cuff links and the like, believing that brotherhood would play a role in the outcome of the debate.

There were a multitude of items both quaint and curious on the evening's warrant, ranging from leaf-plugged storm drains to the removal of certain dead elm trees. Voters were also treated to a dialectic on the rovings of a certain mad dog who had made his activities a nuisance in the shiretown.

And there was considerable discussion over certain roadways that had gone unplowed during the winter months.

The warrant was also fecund with items concerning the maintenance of old burial plots, repairs to fences and even a claim by an elderly gentleman that a bear had destroyed his beehives and was, as a ward of the county seat, the responsibility of this gathering. Holbrook Currier was also appearing as this fellow's counsel.

The hall was swarming with armchair orators, retired judges of probate, born-again fiscal conservatives, defrocked ministers, advocates of holistic medicine, lawyers with lean practices, law students eager for attention, former state senators with time on their hands, former state senator's brothers, disc jockeys, recently released mental patients, drunkards, unpublished poets, retired policemen, antivivisectionists, liberated women, organic farmers, windmill salesmen and the odd socialist.

There was also a substantial representation from that fraternity which finds rural Maine cute—tourists, immigrants, visiting professors, lost skiers, reporters from *The Boston Globe*, television personalities, social scientists, a photographer from *National Geographic* and a covey of do-gooders seeking monies to aid certain Central American nations and various flora and fauna in need of assistance. They had come to view the bumpkin in his lair.

Holbrook Currier had planned a big presentation with various charts, maps and a slide show, along with something called "impact statements" from various experts who will, for a modest fee, testify to the high purpose of one's endeavors, whatever those may be.

But at this point in the frivolities the spirit moved the old showman in Chick Devine, and he leapt to his feet and obtained the floor after having first bested several leather-lunged opponents who were reticent to yield.

Devine's oration, or "philippic," as he was later to call it, was brief but spirited, appealing to those sentiments dearest to the hearts of Maine voters.

The impresario emphasized that he was a Maine native, which brought a great volume of applause, cheering and foot stomping, so that order was not restored in the hall for several minutes, and then only after two or three of Devine's most enthusiastic listeners had been forcedly removed from the hall by the burly Matmen.

At this point in his address Chick Devine climbed up onto the dais and removed his suit coat. He then told the voters that his grand design for Club Maine would not cost the county a plug nickel, which brought more cheering and applause. He vowed that it would bring hundreds of jobs to the unemployment-plagued region.

The cheering at this point increased so much that many of the showman's remarks were inaudible, and cries of "God Bless you, Chick" were heard throughout the hall.

Lastly, Devine promised voters that his plan for Club Maine would increase the size of the deer herd, though he did not elaborate on this phenomenon. He received a thunderous ovation, and the motion to allow the changes in land-use regulations and other matters went sailing through on a voice vote.

The *Abenaki Clarion* reported extensively on the proceedings the following day, running a full account of the evening under the headline, SHOWMAN WOWS VOTERS AND BRINGS DOWN THE HOUSE.

The account also featured a photograph of Chick Devine being carried around the hall on the shoulders of the Matmen.